Joseph Priestley

Letters to the Right Honourable Edmund Burke

Occasioned by his Reflections on the revolution in France

Joseph Priestley

Letters to the Right Honourable Edmund Burke
Occasioned by his Reflections on the revolution in France

ISBN/EAN: 9783337189754

Printed in Europe, USA, Canada, Australia, Japan

Cover: Foto ©Andreas Hilbeck / pixelio.de

More available books at **www.hansebooks.com**

LETTERS

TO

THE RIGHT HONOURABLE

EDMUND BURKE,

OCCASIONED BY HIS

REFLECTIONS

ON THE

REVOLUTION in FRANCE, &c.

By JOSEPH PRIESTLEY, L.L.D. F.R.S.

AC. IMP. PETROP. R. PARIS. HOLM. TAURIN. ITAL. HARLEM. AUREL. MED.
PARIS. CANTAB. AMERIC. ET PHILAD. SOC.

Eloquence may exist without a proportionable degree of wisdom.
Mr. Burke's Reflections, p. 245.

Steady independent minds, when they have an object of so serious a
concern to mankind, as GOVERNMENT, under their contemplation,
will disdain to assume the part of *satyrists* and *declaimers.*
Ibid. p. 187.

BIRMINGHAM,

PRINTED BY THOMAS PEARSON;

AND SOLD BY J. JOHNSON, ST. PAUL'S CHURCH-YARD, LONDON.

MDCCXCI.

(PRICE TWO SHILLINGS AND SIXPENCE.)

PREFACE.

OF the numerous readers, and anfwerers, of Mr. Burke's long expected *Reflections on the Revolution in France*, the attention of the greater part will be chiefly drawn to thofe paffages which more immediately relate to the *civil conflitution* of that kingdom. Thefe I have not neglected. But, what I have more particularly replied to, is what he has advanced on *civil eftablifhments of religion*, which makes no fmall figure in his performance, and which appears to be a fubject not generally underftood.

It is with very fenfible regret that I find Mr. Burke and myfelf on the two oppofite fides of any important queftion, and efpecially that I muft now no longer clafs him among the friends of what I deem to be

the

the cauſe of liberty, *civil* or *religious*, after having, in a pleaſing occaſional inter-
courſe of many years, conſidered him in
this reſpeðable light. In the courſe of
his public life, he has been greatly be-
friended by the Diſſenters, many of whom
were enthuſiaſtically attached to him ; and
we always imagined that he was one on
whom we could depend, eſpecially as he
ſpoke in our favour in the buſineſs of ſub-
ſcription, and he made a common cauſe
with us in zealouſly patronizing the liberty
of America.

That an avowed friend of the American
revolution ſhould be an enemy to that of the
French, which aroſe from the ſame general
principles, and in a great meaſure ſprung
from it, is to me unaccountable. Nor is it
much leſs difficult to conceive how any perſon, who has had America in his eye ſo
long as Mr. Burke muſt neceſſarily have
contemplated it, could be ſo impreſſed, as
he appears to be, in favour of *eccleſiaſtical*
eſtabliſhments. That country he ſees to flou-
riſh

rifh as much as any other in the annals of hiftory, without any civil eftablifhment of religion at all. There he muft fee the civil government goes on very well without it. It neither ftands in need of religion, nor does religion ftand in need of it. For America is fo far from being a country of atheifts and unbelievers, that there is, I doubt not, a ftronger general fenfe of religion there than in any other part of the world.

In America alfo, and indeed in every other part of the known world, except the fouthern part of this particular ifland, Mr. Burke fees all civil offices open to perfons of all religious perfuafions without diftinction, and without any inconvenience having been known to arife from it; and yet here he joins with a bigotted clergy, in rigoroufly confining them to the members of the eftablifhed church. But even *this* is not fo extraordinary as his not fcrupling to clafs all the enemies of eftablifhments with *cheats* and *hypocrites*, as if our opinions were fo

A 3   palpably

palpably abſurd, that no honeſt man could poſſibly entertain them.

Some are diſpoſed to aſcribe this change in Mr. Burke's views and politics, to his reſentment of the treatment of the *coalition* by the Diſſenters. And certainly ſo *ſudden* an union of Mr. Burke and his friends with Lord North, with whom they had been in a ſtate of violent oppoſition during the whole of the American war, did fill the Diſſenters, but not the Diſſenters only (for the ſhock affected the greater part of the nation) with horror. In this it is poſſible they might have judged wrong, liſtening to no *reaſon* againſt the effect of the firſt unfavourable *impreſſion*; but they certainly acted from the beſt principles, an attachment to liberty, virtue, and conſiſtency; and they lamented the fall of Mr. Burke, as that of a friend and a brother.

However, the queſtion before the reader, is not the propriety or impropriety of any particular man's conduct, but the wiſdom

of

of great meafures of government ; as whether it be right, and wife, to connect the
bufinefs of *religion* with that of the *ftate*, in
the manner in which it is done in this country, and whether the French nation is jufti-
fiable in their attempts to change their arbitrary form of government for another which
they deem to be more favourable to their
interefts and natural rights.

The queftion alfo with refpect to *them*,
is not whether they have taken the very beft
methods poffible to gain their end, but whether the thing itfelf was worth their aiming
at, and whether they have been thofe *very
great fools* that Mr. Burke makes them to be.
After all, mankind in general will judge
by the event.   If they fucceed in eftablifhing a free government, they will be ap-
plauded for their *judgment*, as well as for
the *fpirit* that they have fhewn ; and if they
fail, they will be condemned for their precipitancy and folly.   Thus every fuccefsful
revolt is termed a revolution, and every un-
fuccefsful one a rebellion.

If

If the principles that Mr. Burke now advances (though it is by no means with perfect confiftency) be admitted, mankind are always to be governed as they have been governed, without any enquiry into the *nature*, or *origin*, of their governments. The *choice of the people* is not to be confidered, and though their happinefs is aukwardly enough made by him the end of government; yet, having no choice, they are not to be the judges of what is for their good. On thefe principles, the *church*, or the *ftate*, once eftablifhed, muft for ever remain the fame. This is evidently the real fcope of Mr. Burke's pamphlet, the principles of it being, in fact, no other than thofe of *paffive obedience and non-refiftance*, peculiar to the Tories and the friends of arbitrary power, fuch as were echoed from the pulpits of all the high church party, in the reigns of the Stuarts, and of Queen Anne. Let them, however, be produced again, and let us fee in what manner they will be treated by the good fenfe and fpirit of Englifhmen at the prefent day.

After

After the firſt part of theſe letters relating more immediately to the French Revolution were printed, I had an opportunity of ſeeing the *Memoir of the Compte De Lally Tollendal*, of whoſe account of the tranſaction of the ſixth of October, Mr. Burke has availed himſelf ſo much, p. 109, &c. calling him "one of the moſt honeſt, in-"telligent, and eloquent members of the "National Aſſembly." I have particularly compared his account of this Aſſembly, with that of Mr. Burke, p. 24, where he ſays, " I conſider this Aſſembly as nothing "elſe than a voluntary aſſociation of men "who have availed themſelves of circum-"ſtances to ſeize upon the power of the "ſtate, and that they have not the ſanction, "and authority, of the character under "which they firſt met."

Mr. Tollendal's ideas were certainly very different from theſe of Mr. Burke. For, ſpeaking of his being choſen a member of the Aſſembly, he ſays, p. 5, " it was, with-"out doubt, a great occaſion, and a great "work

" work, to concur in the regeneration of
" France, in founding liberty there, and in
" creating laws and manners*!" What,
then, has the National Affembly done, or
attempted to do, more than this, which
Mr. Tollendal clearly conceived to have
been the defign of their meeting? Though
he thought proper to leave this Affembly,
yet he acknowledges, p. 45, that " the
" majority of the perfons who compofed
" it, had the pureft intentions†;" and he
fpeaks in the higheft terms of approbation concerning the *declaration of Rights*,
which was their firft Act. After making
fome objections refpecting the form, more
than the fubftance, he fays, p. 125, " it
" contains all the great principles which
" are the guards of focieties, which main-

* C'étoit, fans doute, une affez grande occafion;
c'étoit un affez grand travail, que de concourir à ré-
générer la France, à y fondre la liberté, & à y créer des
lois & des mœurs.

† Une très petite portion d'individus pourroit ren-
dre inutiles les intentiones pures de la majorité.

" tain

" tain the rights of man, and of his dig-
" nity, and which fecure his tranquility
" and happinefs*." And thefe are thofe
rights of men which Mr. Burke treats with
fo much ridicule.

In order to form a judgment whether the
National Affembly had actually exceeded
their commiffion, or had undertaken more
than was required of them, I alfo looked
into the King of France's *circular letter
for the convocation of the States at Verfailles*,
dated January 24, 1789, as it is contained
in the *New Annual Regifter*, for 1789,
p. 111. According to it, this Affembly
was convened " to eftablifh a fteady, con-
" ftant, and invariable order in every part
" of government, that interefted the hap-

---

* Il eft cependant vrai de dire, que tous les grandes
principes, tous ces principes tutelaires des focietés,
confervateurs des droits de l'homme, & de fa dignité,
protecteurs de fon repos & de fon bonheur, y font ren-
fermés. Je crois que cette declaration pourra être
applaudie, le jour où les troubles qui s'elevoient, pen-
dant que nous la rédigions, feront calmes.

" pinefs

" pinefs of the people, and the profperity
" of the kingdom ; that an effectual re-
" medy might be applied to the diforders
" of the ftate, and that abufes of every kind
" might be reformed and prevented, by good
" and folid means, proper to infure a per-
" manency of the public happinefs."   And
laftly, it is faid to be " for every thing that
" might concern the prefent and future
" wants of the ftate."

Again, in the *King's letter to the Prefi-*
dent of the Affembly, dated May 28, 1789,
he fays, "I cannot fee without pain the
" National Affembly, which I have called
" together, to be concerned with me in the
" new regulation of the kingdom, funk
" into inaction; which if continued, would
" caufe all the hopes which I have formed
" for the happinefs of my people, and the
" benefit of the ftate to prove abortive."

Certainly, therefore, in the opinion of
the King, as well as that of the whole nation, there was a want of a total reform in
the

the conftitution of the French government, and this reform was expected from the National Affembly. This is the very thing which they are endeavouring to effect, and in which they have made confiderable progrefs. What they have done gives the greateft pleafure to the friends of univerfal liberty, though unfortunately it gives pain to Mr. Burke, and fome others.

THE

CONTENTS.

Letter

CONTENTS.

———————

E R R A T A.

N. B. (*b*) signifies from the bottom.

Page 1, l. 7, for *of* read *in.*
  33, l. 5 (*b*) — *term* — *terms.*
  41, l. 7 (*b*) — *with* — *with the.*
  43, l. 4 (*b*) — *the* — *a.*
  45, l. 2 (*b*) — *all* — *of.*
  50, l. 5, — *at* — *as.*
  61, l. 7, — *at* — *up.*
  85, l. 6, — *of* — *out of.*
  92, l. 6, — *unstrained* — *unrestrained.*
  109, l. 7, — *of the* — *of.*
  121, l. 8 (*b*) — *being* — *been.*

LETTERS

EDMUND BURKE.

———————

LETTER I.

Of the general Principles of the French Revolution.

DEAR SIR,

I Do not wonder that the late revolution of the
French government, has excited *your* attention,
and that of a great part of the nation. " It is,"
as you juftly fay, p. 11, " all circumftances taken
" together, the moft aftonifhing that has hitherto
" happened in the world." It is, therefore, a moft
interefting object both to philofophical and practi-
cal politicians. It behoves them to confider the
principles on which it has been made, that if the
conduct of the leaders in the bufinefs has been right,

B   and

and if the fcheme promifes to be beneficial to the country, it may, as far as their fituations are fimilar, be imitated in other countries; and that, if their conduct has been wrong, and the refult of it unpromifing, the example may ferve to deter others from any attempt of the like kind.

But though there is nothing extraordinary in this revolution having excited fo much of your *attention*, I am furprifed that you fhould be fo much *alarmed* and *difturbed* at it. You appear to me not to be fufficiently cool to enter into this ferious difcuflion. Your imagination is evidently heated, and your ideas confufed. The objects before you do not appear in their proper fhapes and colours; and, without denying them, you lofe fight of the great and the leading principles, on which all juft governments are founded, principles which I imagined had been long fettled, and univerfally affented to, at leaft by all who are denominated *whigs*, the friends of our own revolution, and of that which has lately taken place in America. To this clafs of politicians, you have hitherto profeffed to belong, and traces of thefe principles may be perceived in this work of yours.

Notwithftanding " the facrednefs," as you call it, p. 29, " of an hereditary principle of fucceffion," in our government, you allow of " a power of " change in its application in cafes of extreme " emergency;" adding, however, that " the change
" fhould

" fhould be confined to the *peccant part* only." Nor do you deny that the great end and object of all government, that which makes it preferable to a ftate of anarchy, is the good of the people. It is *better* for them, and they are *happier* in a ftate of government. For the fame reafon, you muft allow that that particular form of government, which is beft adapted to promote the happinefs of any people, is the beft for that people.

If you admit thus much, you muft alfo allow that, fince every private perfon is juftified in better-ing his condition, and indeed commended for it; a nation is not to be condemned for endeavouring to better theirs. Confequently, if they find their form of government to be a bad one, whether it was fo originally, or became fo through abufe or accident, they will do very well to change it for a better. A partial change, no doubt, will be preferable to a total one, if a partial change will be fufficient for the purpofe. But if it appear that all attempts to mend an old conftitution would be in vain, and the people prefer a new one, their neighbours have no more bufinefs to find fault with them, than with any individual, who fhould think it more advifeable to pull down an old and inconvenient houfe, and build another from the foundation, rather than lay out his money in repairs. Nations, no doubt, as well as individuals, may judge wrong. They may act pre-

B 2 cipitately,

cipitately, and they may fuffer in confequence of it: but this is only a reafon for caution, and does not preclude a right of judging and acting for themfelves, in the beft manner they can.

" The very idea," you fay, p. 44, " of the fabri- " cation of a new government is enough to fill us " with difguft and horror." It is, no doubt, far from being a thing defirable in itfelf; but it may neverthelefs be neceffary; and for all the evils arif- ing from the change, you fhould blame not the framers of the new government, but the wretched ftate of the old one, and thofe who brought it into that ftate. That fome very material change was wanting in the old government of France, you cannot deny, after allowing, p. 195, that " in that country " the unlimited power of the fovereign over the " perfons of his fubjects, was inconfiftent with law " and liberty." On other occafions, I believe you have expreffed yourfelf in a ftronger manner than this. If *law* and *liberty* were wanting in the old conftitution, the peccant part muft have been the very foundation of it; fo that nothing effectual could have been done fhort of taking down the whole.

If thefe incontrovertible *principles* and *facts* be admitted, I can fee no reafon for your exclaiming fo violently as you do againft the late revolution in France. Befides, whatever has been done, and in whatever manner it has been done, if the nation it-

felf,

felf, whom alone it concerns, do not complain, we have no bufinefs to complain for them, any farther than the intereft we take in the welfare of others, may lead us to feel for the diftreffes which we apprehend their folly and precipitancy may bring upon them. I fhall, however, briefly confider the principal of your objections to this revolution.

You confider the prefent National Affembly of France as ufurpers, affuming a power that does not belong to them. "I can never," you fay, p. 242, " confider this affembly as any thing elfe " than a voluntary affociation of men, who have " availed themfelves of circumftances to feize upon " the power of the ftate. They have not the fanc- " tion and authority of the character under which " they firft met. They have affumed another, of a " very different nature, and have completely al- " tered and inverted all the relations in which they " originally ftood. They do not hold the authority " they exercife under any conftitutional law of the " ftate. They have departed from the inftruc- " tions of the people by whom they were fent, " which inftructions, as the affembly did not act in " virtue of any ancient ufuage or fettled law, were " the fole fource of their authority."

Now, Sir, even allowing this to be true; admitting this National Affembly to have had no regular fummons to meet, or to do any bufinefs at all;

fuppof-

supposing them to have been men who rose out of the earth, or who dropped down from the clouds, or that no body could tell whence they came, and that, without any authority whatever, they took upon themselves to frame a new constitution of government for the French nation; if the nation really approve of it, acquiesce in it, and actually adopt it, it becomes from that time their own act, and the Assembly can only be considered as the proposers and advisers. It is the acquiescence of the people that gives any form of government its proper sanction, and that legalizes it. Changes of government cannot be brought about by established forms and rules, because there is no superior power to prescribe those rules. There are no supreme courts comprehending those great objects. Also, the cases occur so rarely, and they are so unlike to one another, that it would be to no purpose to look for precedents.

Now, that the French revolution is justifiable on this plain principle, is evident from the single circumstance of the National Assembly having continued their sittings without molestation, and from their decrees having been actually obeyed, for something more than a year at least. This Assembly does not consist, I believe, of more than about one thousand persons, and at first they had no army at their command; whereas at present the whole force

of

of the ſtate is in their hands. This force could not have been transferred from the king to them, without the conſent both of the army, and of the nation which ſupports that army. As the nation does not complain of this tranſlation of power, it is evident they do not think themſelves aggrieved, and that the change has been made with their approbation. Here, then, we ſee all the marks of a *legal government*, or a government that is really the *choice of the people*. I do not ſay what difficulties may hereafter ariſe (which if they do, they will probably be the effect of their former government) to induce them to change their opinion. For neither that nation, nor any other, is omniſcient and infallible.

Without examining into the former ſyſtem of government, or the adminiſtration of it, we may take for granted, that it muſt have become extremely odious to the country in general, from the almoſt univerſal, and the very hearty, concurrence with which the revolution was brought about. A whole people is not apt to revolt, till oppreſſion has become extreme, and been long continued, ſo that they deſpair of any other remedy than that deſperate one. The ſtrength of an eſtabliſhed government, eſpecially when it is in few hands, and has a large ſtanding army at its command, is almoſt infinite; ſo that many nations quietly ſuffer every evil, and the country becomes in a manner deſolate,

without

without their making any attempt to relieve themfelves. This is the cafe in all the Turkifh domi-
nions, and is faid to be very nearly fo in Spain and
other countries. Whenever, therefore, we fee a
whole nation, or a great majority of it, rifing as one
man againft an old government, and overturning it,
we may fafely conclude that their provocation was
great, and their caufe good.

An oppreffed people do not, however, in general fee any thing more than what they immediately
feel. All they think of is to fhake off the load which
they can no longer bear; and having thought of nothing but the particular evil that galled them, they
are very apt, in their future fettlement, to guard
againft that only, without attending to the whole of
their new fituation, and the greater evils that may
poffibly arife from it. Whether the French have
done fo or not, time muft difcover. But if the
people in general are well informed, and well difpofed, they may make many experiments of new
forms of government without much inconvenience;
and though beginning with a very imperfect one,
they may adopt a very good one at the laft.

Was it not predicted that the Americans, on
their breaking off from this country, would run into
univerfal confufion, and immediately fall to cutting
one another's throats? But though that difrup-
tion was a violent one, and was effected by a war,

which

which drained all their refources, they never fuffered for want of government. When the war was over they bore very contentedly feveral imperfect and disjointed forms; and now, having taken much time to deliberate on the fubject, they have adopted a more comprehenfive one. But of this they only propofe to make a trial, and if it fhould not anfwer, they will, no doubt, endeavour to improve upon it.

Now, why may not this be the cafe with the French, efpecially as they have no enemies to contend with, and interrupt their proceedings. I do not, I own, diftinctly perceive the wifdom of feveral parts of the frame of government, at prefent adopted by the National Affembly, and many of the remarks that you have made upon it, may, for any thing that I know, be very juft; but not being a judge of their circumftances, and confequently of all their reafons, I prefume that they could not for the prefent do any better. In future time, however, whatever it be that is now deficient may be fupplied. And confidering the apparent ftrength of the ancient French government, and the great numbers that depended upon it (far more, I fhould imagine, than upon our court and miniftry in this country) I wonder that the revolution was brought about with fo much eafe, and fo little bloodfhed.

I am, &c.

LETTER

LETTER II.

*Of some Particulars in the new Constitution of France,
and some Circumstances attending the Dissolution of
the old one.*

DEAR SIR,

IT is very possible that the National Assembly,
having entered upon the business of reforming
the whole state in a very unexpected manner, when
nothing could have been preconcerted, may have
acted injudiciously in more respects than one ; but
allowance should be made for their peculiar circumstances. The opportunity that was given them to
act was sudden, and such as they might in vain
have waited for, if they had done nothing till they
had been prepared to make the most of it. They
did right, therefore, to do the best they could, as
the occasion offered.

They might, for example, have divided themselves into two houses, and, as in this country, have
given each house a negative in all their transactions,
and another to the king. But this might have appeared too hazardous at that time ; and indeed it
is very probable that, upon that plan, nothing ef-

fectual

fectual could have been done at all. But they may adopt this method if they fhould hereafter fee reafon for it. Power is more eafily given than taken away.

That they have nothing of the nature of a *Senate*, as you complain, p. 287, I do not fee; while they ftill retain a king, and allow him to appoint certain minifters of ftate.

They may have left too little power in the hands of the crown; but kingly power is a plant which, having once taken root, is very apt to grow too luxuriant; and this, though lopped, may fprout again. As the French kings had gradually acquired, and grofsly abufed, their power, it is not to be wondered at, if, in the firft inftance, the Affembly fhould have reduced it too low.

You particularly complain, p. 296, of the king not having the power of peace and war. But was ever any power more grofsly abufed than this has been? Infinite have been the evils brought upon whole countries, by princes having it in their power to involve them in war at their pleafure, from motives of perfonal refentment and ambition, or the mere caprice of thofe about them; and in France generally that of their miftreffes.

"There is no other way," you fay, p. 296, " of " keeping other potentates from intriguing diftinct- " ly and perfonally with the members of your af-

" fembly,

" fembly, from intermeddling in all your concerns,
" and fomenting in the heart of your country the
" moft pernicious of all factions ; factions in the
" intereft, and under the direction, of foreign
" powers." But even *this* is nothing, compared
with the evils that ftates have fuffered from the
power of peace and war being in the hands of the
prince, that is, of his minifters ; and cannot foreign
powers intrigue with *them* as well as with the leaders of a popular affembly ? Did not the court of
France intrigue with the miniftry of our Charles II.
and is it not always done, more or lefs, by all am-
baffadors and their agents in all foreign courts ? But
if any people was fairly reprefented in a National
Affembly, fo that their real interefts fhould be better
confulted, caufes of war would feldom occur, and
confequently there would be but little temptation to
foreigners to intermeddle in their concerns. For it
has been peace or war that has been the chief fubject of the intrigues that you complain of.

The moft ferious difficulty that appears to me
to threaten the French government, arifes from
their *debts*, a difficulty brought upon them by their
former government, and which indeed made it
impoffible to go on any farther with it. This,
therefore, is a difficulty that does not neceffarily
attend the formation of the new government, but
has been occafioned by the unwillingnefs of the pre-

fent

fent governors, that thofe who have had confidence in the ftate, fhould fuffer from the errors of their predeceffors. It is the cafe of an heir, who will put himfelf to great inconvenience to pay the debts of a profligate anceftor.

You cavil, among other things, at the low rank of the members of the National Affembly; faying, p. 61, " That the majority are of the inferior, un-
" learned, mechanical, merely inftrumental, mem-
" bers of the profeffion of the law," that is, fuch as our attornies. " From the moment," you fay, " I
" read the lift, I faw diftinctly, and very nearly as
" it has happened, all that was to follow. It was
" not to be expected," you fay, p. 63, "that
" they would attend to the ftability of property,
" whofe exiftence had always depended upon what-
" ever rendered property queftionable, ambiguous,
" and obfcure."

I fhall not call in queftion your gift of prophecy. It may be your peculiar talent to fee all events, paft, prefent, and to come, in their moft concealed caufes, nor fhall I queftion what you affert to be a fact. But of whomfoever the National Affembly of France confifts, there cannot well be a doubt of their being a truer reprefentation of the French nation than our Houfe of Commons, becaufe there cannot well be a worfe, being in the opinion of moft people, I doubt not, as well as that of Dr. Price, a mere *mockery of reprefentation,*

reprefentation, notwithftanding the influence of thofe caufes which I acknowledge to give it the effect of a much better reprefentation.

It fignifies very little out of what clafs of men the members of the National Affembly were chofen, fince they muft have been perfons in whom their conftituents thought they could beft confide. But if your reafoning be good, that lawyers, " whofe ex-
" iftence depends upon rendering property queftion-
" able, ambiguous, and obfcure," will not attend to the ftability of property, where is our policy in raifing fuch men to the rank of judges? We do not think our property lefs fafe in their hands, becaufe they have always lived by what has been called the *glorious uncertainty of the law.* The firft American Congrefs, I very well remember, was faid to con-fift chiefly of lawyers; nor is it to be wondered at that it fhould be fo; lawyers, who have the talent and the habit of fpeaking in public, being generally confpicuous characters in all places. The ftudy of the law, moreover, leads them to underftand the conftitution of the country, and their profeffion gives them a knowledge of mankind, and the habits of bufinefs. If the lawyers of France do as well as the lawyers of America, they will foon wipe away the reproach they may now lie under, and become the ob-ject of refpect, perhaps of dread, to thofe who at pre-fent defpife them.

It

It is amufing to compare the fentiments of different writers on the fame fubject, and to obferve in how different a light the fame thing appears to different minds. I cannot give a better illuftration of this, than by quoting what Dr. Ramfay, in his *Hiftory of the American Revolution*, fays of the firft Congrefs, as a contraft to what you fay of the National Affembly of France.

" Of the whole number of deputies which form-
" ed the Continental Congrefs of 1774, one half
" were lawyers; gentlemen of that profeffion had
" acquired the confidence of the inhabitants by their
" exertions in the common caufe. The previous
" meafures in the refpective provinces, had been
" planned and carried into effect more by lawyers
" than by any other order of men. Profeffionally
" taught the rights of the people, they were among
" the foremoft to defcry every attack made on
" their liberties. Bred in the habits of public fpeak-
" ing, they made a diftinguifhed figure in the meet-
" ings of the people, and were particularly able to
" explain to them the tendency of the late acts of
" parliament. Exerting their abilities and influ-
" ence in the caufe of their country, they were re-
" warded with its confidence," vol. 1. p. 134.

The miftakes you have fallen into, with refpect to the prefent government of France, I am inform-ed are grofs, and your cenfures founded on them,

ω

of courſe, miſplaced. You particularly amuſe your-ſelf and your readers with the diviſion of the coun-try, p. 254, into ſquares, and a ſub-diviſion of ſquares within ſquares, which has no exiſtence but in your own imagination, the actual diviſion of the country being no more ſquares than our counties.

Taking it for granted, that the preſent members of the National Aſſembly are not eligible into the next, you deduce many alarming conſequences from ſuch an ill-judged meaſure. But the meaſure is your own, not theirs ; the preſent members be-ing as eligible as any others, and, it is generally ſuppoſed, that a great majority of them have given ſo much ſatisfaction to their conſtituents, that they will not fail to be re-elected. As you took ſo much time in preparing your publication for the preſs, you would have done well to have employed part of it in procuring better information. How-ever, your miſtakes will be the means of our get-ting more correct accounts of the real ſtate of facts; and if any of your cenſures on the new conſtitution of France be juſt, they may be an uſeful and ſea-ſonable leſſon to the great actors in the ſcene ; who, I doubt not, will readily learn what they can, even from an enemy.

You make the moſt tragical repreſentation of the degraded ſtate of the preſent king of France, calling it, p. 99, " the moſt horrid, atrocious, and

" afflicting

" afflicting spectacle, that perhaps ever was exhibit-
" ed to the pity and indignation of mankind," considering him as a person who received his crown,
with all its powers, from his anceftors, and who
had himself done nothing to deferve the treatment
that he met with. Admitting this, if by a fucceffion
of incroachments, the power of *the crown itself* had
long been enormous, fhould that be continued, to
the terror and diftrefs of the country, for the fake
of the innocent head that happens to wear it. And,
after all, what has this king fuffered ? He is ftill the
firft in rank, wealth, and power of any perfon in
France. If you fay that this power is only nominal,
I anfwer that the power of the moft arbitrary princes
is little more. They are, in general, only inftruments in the hands of thofe who are about them.
As to doing what a man really wifhes to do, the
laft king of France had very little of it; and in
general, the higher any man ftands in the order of
fociety, the lefs power he has of doing what he
really likes, and the more of his time he fpends in
doing what he had rather wifh not to do, than other
men.

You make a ftill more lamentable defcription of
the indignities offered to the queen of France ; and
on this fubject you give the moft unbounded fcope to
your eloquence*, as if you were her *knight,* pledged

---

* I am informed by a gentleman who was at Paris during the
whole of thefe tranfactions, that there is no truth at all in what

to defend her honour.   Now, such is the natural
prepoffeffion of mankind, at leaft in this part of the
world (in which the French nation has generally
been confidered as foremoft) in favour of the female fex, and efpecially in exalted ftations, that I
think it will not be eafy to account for the fall of
this queen from the height of popularity, to the abhorrence and contempt into which, you tell us, fhe
is funk, without fuppofing fomething very material
to her prejudice, though I do not pretend to fay
what that is.   And if fhe was that intriguing woman, and that enemy to their liberties, that the
French nation in general imagine her to have been,
fhe may think herfelf fortunate, in fuch a revolution
as this has been, to have efcaped with life.   But,
after all, is the liberty and happinefs of a whole nation to be facrificed to female beauty and complai-
fance ?

Objects appear in very different lights to different
perfons, according to their refpective fituations, and
the opportunities they have of obferving them.   To
you, Sir, feventeen years ago, the queen of France,
then the Dauphinefs, appeared in all her fplendour,
like " the morning ftar," p. 112, decorating the

Mr. Burke fays of the queen's bedchamber being broke into, or
the centinel killed.   Nothing of the kind, he fays, was ever heard
of till a confiderable time after the event, and the report arofe
from the Ariftocrates.

face

face of heaven. To the French themselves, at that time, she probably appeared in the same light; but in the course of so many years progress, she has appeared to them to be nothing better than *a comet*, foreboding every disaster, and bringing desolation and ruin on their country. You saw nothing but the fine features, and imagined them to belong to a Venus, a Juno, or a Pallas. The French, it seems, have discovered the *snaky hair*, and find her to be a mere Medusa; and the ten thou- " sand swords," that you say were then ready "to leap " from their scabbards to avenge even a look that " threatened her with insult," would now be drawn against any who would defend her conduct.

You will probably say that something, at least, should have been *proved* against the queen of France, as well as against the king. But where, Sir, was the court of law, or justice, in which such a suit could be instituted ? When there are no ordinary means of redressing grievances, people who feel them, and have no other remedy, will have recourse to extraordinary ones; and if thirty millions find their interests incompatible with that of a few, they, of course, being the judges, will not hesitate to decide for themselves, and carry that decision into execution. In this they will, no doubt, proceed *irregularly*. But you, Sir, should have been upon the spot, and have told them how to proceed in that

grave

grave and *decorous manner*, in which you now fay
they ought to have acted on this great occafion;
and at the fame time have obtained effectual redrefs
of their grievances. For without this, they would
have done worfe than nothing.

Kings and minifters of ftate are alone refponfible
for all the confufion and bloodfhed which attend
thofe revolutions which their abufe of power has
rendered neceffary. They choak up the ordinary
channels of juftice, and then complain that it over-
flows its bounds, and that the country is deluged
by it. They who firft raife a ftorm are anfwerable
for all the devaftation that it may make.

You lay to the charge of the National Affembly
what, it is evident, they never authorifed, and what,
I doubt not, they condemn and regret, even more
than you do. " Their cruelty, you fay, p. 58, has
" not been even the bafe refult of fear. It has been
" the effect of their fenfe of perfect fafety, in au-
" thorifing treafons, robberies, rapes, affaffinations,
" flaughters, and burnings, throughout their har-
" raffed land. But the caufe of all was plain from
" the beginning. This unforced choice, this fond
" election, of evil, would appear perfectly unac-
" countable, if we did not confider the compofition
" of the National Affembly, &c."

This, Sir, is charging upon the National Affembly every outrage committed by Frenchmen (and
more

more, I believe, than ever were committed by them)
which were any way connected with the revolution.
But is this equitable? Should any thing be laid to
the charge of any man, or any body of men, to
which they were no way acceffary, by their concurrence at the time, or their approbation afterwards? Was the execution of perfons particularly
obnoxious to the populace, and effected by the populace, to be afcribed to the National Affembly?
Or were the infults which you have fo pathetically
defcribed, as offered to your adorable queen of
France, done by the orders of that body? You
muft know that they were as innocent of them as
the parliament of Great Britain, or as yourfelf.
When any murder is committed, is the firft perfon
that you chufe to lay hold of, the guilty perfon?

In the fame rafh and indifcriminate manner you
defcribe Dr. Price as exulting in the above-mentioned horrid outrages, which, I dare fay, give him
much more ferious concern than they do you, and
for a very obvious reafon. He wifhes to recommend the revolution, and therefore is forry for every thing that difgraces it; whereas you wifh to
difcredit it, and are evidently not difpleafed with
any circumftance that favours your purpofe. Dr.
Price rejoices in the *good*, and you moft uncandidly
reprefent him as rejoicing in the *evil* that has neceffarily accompanied it.

I am, DEAR SIR, yours, &c.

LETTER III.

Of the Nature of Government, and the Rights of Men and of Kings.

DEAR SIR,

CONSIDERING how much has been written on the fubject of government fince the Revolution in this country, an event which more than any thing elfe contributed to open the eyes of Englifhmen, with refpect to the true principles of it, it is not a little extraordinary that any man of reading and reflexion, as you are, fhould depart from them fo much as you have done.

To vindicate this Revolution, Lord Somers, Bifhop Hoadley, Mr. Locke, and many others, have laid it down as a maxim, that all power in any ftate is derived from the people, and that the great object of all government, is the public good. As a confequence from thefe fundamental principles, they maintain that all magiftrates, being originally appointed by the people, are anfwerable to them for their conduct in office, and removeable at their pleafure. The right of refifting an oppreffive go-

I

vernment,

vernment, that is, fuch as the people fhall deem to be oppreffive, they hold moft facred.

You, Sir, do not directly, and in fo many words, deny thefe great principles of all government, or the general conclufion drawn from them. In fact, you admit them all, when you allow, p. 87, that " civil " fociety is made for the advantage of man." But you advance what is really inconfiftent with thefe leading principles, and you would tie up our hands from making any effectual ufe of them. You feem to have forgotten what you muft have formerly learned; but it is too late for *us* to go to fchool again, and relearn the firft elements of political fcience. What our predeceffors took great pains to *prove*, we now receive as *axioms*, and without hefitation act upon them.

To make the *public good* the ftandard of right or wrong, in whatever relates to fociety and government, befides being the moft natural and rational of all rules, has the farther recommendation of being the eafieft of application. Either what *God has ordained*, or what *antiquity* authorifes, may be very difficult to afcertain; but what regulation is moft conducive to the *public good*, though not always without its difficulties, yet in general it is much more eafy to determine. But fuppofe a nation fhould never have had a free government, or could not prove that they ever had one, are they

C 4

for

for that reafon always to continue flaves ? Would
it be unlawful, or wrong, in the Turks to do what
the French nation has now done ?

You treat with ridicule the idea of the *rights of
men*, and fuppofe that mankind, when once they
have entered into a ftate of fociety, neceffarily
abandon all their proper *natural rights*, and thence-
forth have only fuch as they derive from fociety.
" As to the fhare of power," you fay, p. 87, " au-
" thority and direction, which each individual
" ought to have in the management of the ftate,
" that I muft deny to be among the direct original
" rights of man in civil fociety ; for I have in my
" contemplation the civil, focial man, and no other.
" It is a thing to be fettled by convention."

But what does this *convention* refpect, befide
the fecure enjoyment of fuch *advantages*, or *rights*, as
have been ufually termed *natural*, as life, liberty,
and property, which men had *from nature*, without
focieties, or artificial combinations of men? Men
cannot, furely, be faid to *give up* their natural rights
by entering into a compact for the better *fecuring* of
them? And if they make a wife compact, they will
never wholly exclude themfelves from all fhare in
the adminiftration of their government, or fome control over it.   For without this their ftipulated rights
would be very infecure.

However,

However, ſhould any people be ſo unwiſe as to leave the whole adminiſtration of their government, without any expreſs right of control, in the hands of their magiſtrates; if thoſe magiſtrates do not give the people what they deem to be an equivalent for what they gave up for the accommodation of others, they are certainly at liberty to conſider the original compact as broken. They then revert to a ſtate of nature, and may enter into a new ſtate of ſociety, and adopt a new form of government, in which they may make better terms for themſelves.

It is one of the moſt curious paradoxes in this work of yours, which abounds with them, that the rights of men above-mentioned, called by you, p. 91, " the pretended rights of the French theoriſts, are " all extremes, and in proportion as they are me- " taphyſically true, they are morally and politically " falſe." Now by *metaphyſically* true can only be meant *ſtrictly* and *properly* true, and how this can be in any ſenſe *falſe*, is to me incomprehenſible. If the above-mentioned rights be the *true*, that is the *juſt*, and *reaſonable* rights of men, they ought to be pro- vided for in all ſtates, and all forms of government; and if they be not, the people have juſt cauſe to complain, and to look out for ſome mode of re- dreſs.

You ſtrongly reprobate the doctrine of *kings being the choice of the people*, a doctrine advanced, but not
" firſt

firſt advanced, by Dr. Price, in his Revolution Sermon. " This doctrine,'' you ſay, p. 17, " as ap-
" plied to the prince now on the Britiſh throne, is
" either nonſenſe, and therefore neither true nor
" falſe, or it affirms a moſt unfounded, dangerous,
" illegal, and unconſtitutional poſition. According
" to this ſpiritual doctor of politics, if his majeſty
" does not owe his crown to the choice of his peo-
" ple, he is no *lawful* king, &c.''

On the ſame principle you equally reprobate the
doctrine of the king being the *ſervant of the people*,
whereas the law, as you ſay, p. 41, calls him *our
ſovereign lord the king* *. But ſince you allow, ibid.
that " kings are in one ſenſe, undoubtedly, the ſer-
" vants of the people, becauſe their power has no
" other rational end than that of the general ad-
" vantage,'' it is evident that it is only Dr. Price's
words that you quarrel with. Your *ideas* are, in
fact, the very ſame with his, though you call his
doctrine, p. 35, not only *unconſtitutional*, but *ſedi-
tious*; adding, that " it is now publicly taught,
" avowed, and printed,'' whereas it was taught,
avowed, and even printed, before either you or Dr.
Price were born.

---

* This title of *ſovereign lord*, derived from the Feudal ſyſtem,
given to a king of England, is by no means agreeable to the nature
and ſpirit of our preſent conſtitution, which is a *limited monarchy*,
and not *unlimited* as that title implies. Our only proper *ſovereign*
is the parliament.

Has

Has not the chief magiſtrate in every country, as well as the chief officer in every town, a certain *duty* to perform, with certain emoluments, and *privileges*, allowed him in confideration of the proper diſcharge of that duty? And if the town officer, though having chief authority in his diſtrict, yet, in confequence of being appointed and paid for his fervices by the town, is never confidered in any other light than that of the *ſervant of the town*, is not the chief magiſtrate in any country, let him be called *fovereign*, *king*, or what you pleafe (for that is only a name) the *ſervant of the people?* What real difference can there be in the two cafes? They each diſcharge a certain duty, and have a certain ſtipulated reward for it. The office being *hereditary*, makes no real difference. In our laws, and thofe of other nations, there are precedents cnow of men's whole eſtates being confiſcated for crimes; and this of courſe excludes the heir.

If, as you expreſsly acknowledge, the only rational end of the " power of a king is the *general advantage*, that is, the *good of the people*, muſt not the people be, of courſe, the judges, whether they derive advantage from him and his government or not, that is, whether they be well or ill *ſerved* by him? Though, there is no expreſs, there is, you muſt acknowledge a virtual, *contract between the king and the people*. This, indeed, is particularly mentioned

tioned in the Act which implies the abdication of king James, though you fay, p. 38, it is *too guarded and too circumftantial*; and what can this contract be, but a ftipulation for protection, &c. on the part of the king, and allegiance on the part of the people? If, therefore, inftead of *protection*, they find *oppreffion*, certainly allegiance is no longer due. Hence, according to common fenfe, and the principles of the Revolution, the right of a fubject to refift a tyrant, and dethrone him; and what is this, but in other words, fhocking as they may found to your ears, difmiffing, or *cafhiering a bad fervant*, as a perfon who had abufed his truft?

So fafcinating is the fituation in which our kings are placed, that it is of great importance to remind them of the true relation they bear to the people, or, as they are fond of calling them, *their people*. They are too apt to imagine that their rights are independent of the will of the people, and confequently that they are not accountable to them for any ufe they may make of their power; and their numerous dependents, and efpecially the clergy, are too apt to adminifter this pleafing intoxicating poifon. This was the ruin of the Stuarts, and it is a danger that threatens every prince, and every country, from the fame quarter. Your whole book, Sir, is little elfe than a vehicle for the fame poifon, inculcating, but inconfiftently enough, a principle

of

of *respect for princes*, independent of their being originally the choice of the people, as if they had
fome natural and indefeafible right to reign over
us, they being born to command, and we to obey;
and then, whether the origin of this power be divine, or have any other fource independent of the
people, it makes no difference to us.

With the fuperftitious refpect for kings, and the
fpirit of chivalry, which nothing but an age of extreme barbarifm recommended, and which civilization has banifhed, you feem to think that every
thing great and dignified has left us, " Never, ne-
" ver more," you fay, p. 113, " fhall we behold
" that generous loyalty to rank and fex, that proud
" fubmiffion, that dignified obedience, that fubor-
" dination of the heart, that kept alive even in fer-
" vitude itfelf the fpirit of an exalted freedom.
" The unbought grace of life, the cheap defence of
" nations, the nurfe of manly fentiment and he-
" roic enterprize, is gone. It is gone; that fenfibi-
" lity of principle, that chaftity of honour, which
" felt a ftain like a wound, which infpired courage
" whilft it mitigated ferocity, which enobled what-
" ever it touched, and under which vice itfelf loft
" half its evil, by lofing all its groffnefs."

This is perhaps the moft admired paffage in your
whole performance; but it appears to me, that in
a great pomp of *words*, it contains but few *ideas*,
and

and some of them inconsistent and absurd. So different also are men's feelings, from the difference, no doubt, of our educations, and the different sentiments we voluntarily cherish through life, that a situation which gives you the idea of *pride*, gives me that of *meanness*. You are proud of what, in my opinion, you ought to be ashamed, the idolatry of a fellow creature, and the abasement of yourself. It discovers a disposition from which no " manly " sentiment, or heroic enterprize" can be expected. I submit to a king, or to any other civil magistrate, because the good order of society requires it, but I feel no *pride* in that *submission*; and the " sub- " ordination of my heart," I reserve for *character* only, not for *station*. As a citizen, the object of my respect is *the nation*, and *the laws*. The *magistrates*, by whatever name they are called, I respect only as the confidential servants of the nation, and the administrators of the laws.

These sentiments, just in themselves, and favouring of no superstition, appear to me to become men, whom nature has made equal, and whose great object, when formed into societies, it should be to promote their common happiness. I am proud of feeling myself *a man among men*, and I leave it you, Sir, to be " proud of your *obedience*, and to keep alive," as well as you can, " in servitude itself the spirit of " an exalted freedom." I think it much easier, at least, to be preserved *out* of a state of servitude than

in

in it. You take much pains to gild your chains, but they are chains ftill.

If, Sir, you profefs this " generous loyalty, this " proud fubmiffion, this dignified obedience, and " this fubordination of the heart," both to *rank and sex*, how concentrated and exalted muft be the fentiment, where rank and fex are united! What an *exalted freedom* would you have felt, had you had the happinefs of being a fubject of the Emprefs of Ruffia; your fovereign, being then a *woman?* Fighting under her aufpices, you would no doubt, have been the moft puiffant of knights errant, and her redoubted champion, againft the whole Turkifh empire, the fovereign of which is only a *man.*

" It is to no purpofe to fay," as you do, p. 19, " that the king of Great Britain reigns at this day " by a fixed rule of fucceffion, according to the " laws of his country, and that he holds his crown " in contempt of the choice of the Revolution fo- " ciety, which has not a fingle vote for a king " among them, either individually or collectively ;" when you acknowledge that " all the kingdoms " of Europe were, at a remote period, elective," and that " the prefent king holds his rank no " longer than while the legal conditions of the com- " pact of fovereignty are performed by him." This, Sir, is granting all that we, feditious as our doctrine is, contend for. Here is, according to yourfelf,

yourfelf, a certain *condition* on which kings reign. If, therefore, that condition be not performed, the obligation of allegiance is difcharged.

Though we do not chufe any particular king, the nation originally chofe to be *governed by kings*, with fuch limitations, with refpect to their duty and prerogatives, as they then chofe to prefcribe. And whether the departure from the original and proper duty of a king be made at once, or by degrees, which has generally been the cafe; and though the people may have been reftrained by their circumftances from checking the incroachments of their kings, the *right* of doing it muft ever remain inherent in them. They muft always have a power of refuming what themfelves gave, when the condition on which it was given is not performed. They can furely recal a truft that has been abufed, and reinftate themfelves in their former fituation, or in a better, if they can find one.

If there be, what you allow, a *compact of fovereignty*, who are the *parties*, but the *people* and the *king*; and if the compact be broken on his fide, are not the rank and the privileges, which he held upon the condition of obferving the term of the compact, forfeited ? " The rule of fucceffion," you fay, " is " according to the laws of his country." But what, according to yourfelf, is the origin of both our common and ftatute law ?

" Both

" Both thefe defcriptions of law," you fay, p. 28,
" are of the fame force, and are derived from an
" equal authority, emanating from the common
" agreement, and original compact of the ftate
" (*communi fponfione reipublicæ*) and as fuch are
" equally binding on king and people too, as long
" as the terms are obferved, and they continue the
" the fame body politic." Laws, then, not com-
ing down from heaven, but being made by men,
may alfo be changed by them; and what is a *conftitution of government*, but the *greater laws* of the
ftate ? Kings, therefore, as well as the people, may
violate thefe laws, by which they are equally bound,
and if other violators of law be punifhable, by de-
gradation or otherwife, why fhould kings be excepted ? Are *their* violations of the law or the conftitution, lefs injurious to the commonwealth than
thofe of other tranfgreffors ? Let the punifhment of
kings be as *grave and decorous*, p. 23, as you pleafe,
but let juftice, fubftantial juftice, be done.

I am, DEAR SIR,

Yours, &c.

D

LETTER IV.

Of the Revolution in England compared with that in France.

DEAR SIR,

IT is impoffible to confider the late Revolution in France without having in our eye that which took place in England in 1688. This has had fo much of the cordial approbation of all claffes of people here, at leaft all thofe who are denominated *whigs*, that you found yourfelf under the neceffity of approving of it. But you wifh to diftinguifh between the principles on which the great actors in that memorable event proceeded, and thofe of the National Affembly in France. The promoters of the Englifh Revolution, you would have us underftand, were not guided by any view to the *natural* (or, as you affect to call them, the *chimerical*) *rights of men*, but were influenced by a regard to rights fanctioned by *ancient poffeffion*, and confequently that their example furnifhes no authority for any people to chufe their own governors, or to difmifs them for mifconduct.

You

You appeal to *Lord Somers*, p. 27, for the principles of the English Revolution. Let his writings, then, explain his sentiments on the nature of government. Now the very title page of a tract generally ascribed to him, entitled, *the Judgment of whole Kingdoms and Nations concerning the Rights, Power, and Prerogative of Kings, and the Rights, Privileges, and Properties of the People*, asserts, that " all magistrates and governors proceed from the " people." This he proves at large in the course of the work, in which he shows, as an inference from this great principle, that the people, when oppressed, are justifiable in relieving themselves by a change of their governors, or of their government; exploding, in a variety of lights, the slavish doctrine, to use his own terms, of *passive obedience and loyalty*.

One of the most extraordinary of your assertions, with respect to the Revolution in England, is the following, " So far," you say, p. 27, " is it " from being true, that we acquired a right by the " Revolution to elect our kings, that if we had " possessed it before, the English nation did at that " time most solemnly renounce and abdicate it for " themselves, and for all their posterity, for ever." But could they seriously mean to bind their posterity from ever doing again what they themselves then did? Did they not by changing the natural

D 2 succession

succeſſion of the kings of this realm, actually *exerciſe* the right of chuſing kings, declaring what deſcription of perſons ſhould from that time ſucceed to the crown? And what any one parliament did, a ſucceeding one might, no doubt, undo.

But that no ſuch thing as a renunciation of a right to do any thing of this kind, was really meant by the legiſlature of that age, is evident from the Act of the ſixth of Queen Anne, pointed out to Dr. Price, by Lord Stanhope, from which it appears that your aſſertion is even nothing leſs than *high treaſon.* The words of the Act are as follows, " If any perſon ſhall, by writing or printing, main- " tain, and affirm, that the kings or queens of this " realm, with and by the authority of Parliament, " are not able to make laws and ſtatutes of ſufficient " validity, to limit the crown, and the deſcent, inhe- " ritance, and government thereof, every ſuch per- " ſon ſhall be guilty of high treaſon."

Far am I from wiſhing to bring you into any ſerious inconvenience by repreſenting you as having offended againſt the laws of your country; but I wiſh it may ſerve as a hint, to pay more attention to the great principles of our conſtitution, as well as to the univerſal principles of government, and the *rights of men,* offenſive as the term may be to you, for the future.

You

You fay, p. 31. "The gentlemen of the *fociety* *"for revolutions"* (as you contemptuoufly call it) " fee nothing of that in 1688, but the deviation " from the conftitution; and they take the devia- " tion from the principle, for the principle." Let us then confider the fimple *fact*, that we may dif- cover the true *principle* of the proceeding, and exa- mine the juftice of your complaint. A king had abufed his truft, and, in the conftruction of the re- maining governing powers of the country, had virtu- ally *abdicated the government*. According to the eftablifhed rule of fucceffion, his fon fhould have fucceeded him, but they apprehended the fame evils from the fon, which they had experienced from the father, and likewife from all princes of the fame defcription with the father, that is, all who fhould profefs the Roman Catholic religion. They therefore, made a law to exclude all fuch princes, and fixed the fucceffion in the neareft Proteftant line. But, in conjunction with the firft of this line, they chofe a perfon entirely foreign to it, who had no legal pretenfions to the crown at all, being only the hufband of Queen Mary, as Prince George of Denmark was of Queen Anne.

Here, then, was a *choice* made, both of a par- ticular king *pro tempore*, and alfo of *a new line of fuc- ceffion* for future kings. Certainly, therefore, if the conduct of our anceftors in that period be any pre-

D 3   cedent

cedent for future proceedings, it authorizes the people of this country not only to make any change in the rule of fucceffion to the crown, but to do whatever they fhall think neceffary for the redrefs of their grievances. This was unqueftionably the proper *reafon, motive, principle,* or *rule,* of their conduct; and to act upon it in any future time cannot with propriety be called taking " the deviation from " their principle for the principle." To do any thing elfe that fhall be deemed neceffary to remove any prefent evils, and to prevent the recurrence of them, would be doing no more than they would have done in our circumftances.

Confidering the reverence that is always paid to whatever is *ancient,* it is certainly wife in any nation to preferve old inftitutions as long as they are tolerable, becaufe the people will bear with them better than with new ones. This principle no doubt, influenced our anceftors at the Revolution, and at other times. They contented themfelves with removing the preffing grievance, and kept as near to the ancient fyftem as they could. At the Revolution, there was no occafion for any thing more, at leaft the country would not bear any thing more, than a deviation from the line of fucceffion to the crown, leaving the Popifh, and adopting the Proteftant line. But if more had been wanted, they would certainly have done more.

You

You call the Revolution, p. 24, "an act of ne-
"ceſſity." But, what was it that made it necef-
ſary? On what *political principle* was the neceſſity
founded? Was it not deemed neceſſary becauſe
the people apprehended that their liberties, and con-
ſequently their happineſs, were endangered by the
meaſures of the king; and therefore, though, as you
juſtly ſay, p. 44, " a revolution is the laſt reſource
" of the thinking and the good," it was what they
found themſelves driven to. It was the leſs of two
evils which they had in proſpect; and what they did
they thought to be neceſſary for the removal, and
prevention, of the evil. And on the ſame *principle*
that they changed the order of ſucceſſion, they
would have changed the whole frame of the government. Had they apprehended *government by
kings* in general to be as great a grievance as that
by Popiſh kings, they would have aboliſhed kingly
government altogether, and this country would now
have been a republic.

When ever circumſtances have been favourable
to greater changes, wiſe nations have not failed to
adopt them. When America was driven, as you
will allow (for at that time you were very active in
the buſineſs, and many a time have I, with ſingular
ſatisfaction, heard you plead the cauſe of American
liberty) by the oppreſſion of this country, to break
entirely from it, the Americans, ſenſible of more

evils

evils attending their former government, than our ancestors at the revolution, ventured to do a great deal more, and set a glorious example to France, and to the world. They formed a completely new government on the principles of *equal liberty*, and the *rights of men*, "without nobles," as Dr. Price said, "without bishops, and without a king," which, indeed, the Dutch, after their separation from the Spanish monarchy, did in a great measure before them. If arbitrary princes tremble at these great *examples* (at the very idea of which you yourself, as if you were a part of royalty, and appertaining to it, tremble) it is time that they who so long have made others tremble, should, in their turn, tremble themselves. But let the *people* rejoice. It will either make their princes keep within bounds, or encourage them to hope that the time of their deliverance is at hand.

That all persons have not the same dread of revolutions which has seized on you, and that the genuine principles of the Revolution are still preserved, and taught in this country, will appear from the following extracts from *Mr. Paley's Principles of Moral and political Philosophy*, with which I shall close this letter.

" *Government may be too secure.* The greatest ty-
" rants have been those, whose titles were the most
" unquestioned. Whenever, therefore, the opinion
" of

" of right becomes too predominant and fuperftiti-
" ous, it is·abated by *breaking the cuftom.* Thus
" the Revolution broke the *cuftom of fucceffion*, and
" thereby moderated both in the prince and people,
" thofe lofty notions of hereditary right, which in
" the one were become a continual temptation to
" tyranny, and difpofed the other to invite fervi-
" tude, by undue compliances and dangerous con-
" ceffions." p. 411, Quarto Edition.

" The true reafon why mankind hold in detefta-
" tion the memory of thofe who have fold their li-
" berty to a tyrant, is, that together with their own,
" they fold commonly, or endangered, the liberty
" of others ; which certainly they had no right to
" difpofe of." p. 77.

" No ufage, law, or authority whatever, is fo
" binding, that it need or ought to be continued,
" when it may be changed with advantage to the
" community. The family of the prince, the or-
" der of fucceffion, the prerogative of the crown,
" the form and parts of the legiflature, together
" with refpective powers, office, duration, and mu-
" tual dependency of the feveral parts, are all only
" fo many *laws*, mutable like other laws, whenever
" expediency requires, either by the ordinary act of
" the legiflature, or if the occafion deferve it, by
" the interpofition of the people. Thefe points are
" wont to be approached with a kind of awe, they
　　　　　　　　　　　　　　　　　　　　" are

" are reprefented to the mind as principles of the
" conftitution, fettled by our anceftors, and being
" fettled to be no more committed to innovation
" or debate, as foundations never to be ftirred; as
" the terms and conditions of the focial compact,
" to which every citizen of the ftate has engaged
" his fidelity, by virtue of a promife, which he
" cannot now recal. Such reafons have no place
" in our fyftem : to us, if there be any good rea-
" fon for treating thefe with more deference and
" refpect than other laws, it is either the advan-
" tage of the prefent conftitution of government
" which reafon muft be of different force in different
" countries) or becaufe, in all countries, it is of im-
" portance, that the form and ufage of governing
" be acknowledged and underftood, as well by the
" governors as the governed, and becaufe the fel-
" domer it is changed the more it will be refpected
" by both fides." p. 426.

I am, DEAR SIR,

Yours, &c.

LETTER V.

Of the Revolution Society in England, and Mr. Burke's
Reflexions on Dr. Price.

DEAR SIR,

YOU are exceedingly offended at the conduct of the Revolution Society in England, for sending congratulations to the National Affembly in France. " I fhould think it," you fay, p. 6, " at " leaft improper and irregular, to open a formal " public correfpondence with the actual govern- " ment of a foreign nation, without the exprefs au- " thority of the government under which I live." You think it was done " under an equivocal de- " fcription, which to many, unacquainted with " our ufages, might make the addrefs appear as " the act of perfons in fome fort of a corporate bo- " dy, acknowledged by the laws of the kingdom, " and authorifed to fpeak the fenfe of fome part of " it. It is the policy," you fay, p. 7, " that has " very much the complexion of a fraud."

But what occafion could there be to afk leave of the government of one country to fend an addrefs

I   to

to that of another, unleſs it had been *affeƈted* by the correſpondence ; and in *this* caſe the Engliſh government had nothing more to do with the tranſaƈtion than any private individual in the country. Was any thing ſaid by the Revolution Society, *in the name* of the government of this country, or was the latter at all pledged to do one thing or another in the buſineſs ?

As to ſuch a reſpeƈtable body of men as the National Aſſembly of France noticing the addreſs of thoſe who compoſe the Revolution Society in England ; it is nothing new or uncommon, either for ſmall bodies of men to addreſs large ones, or for large ſocieties to notice ſuch addreſſes ; and what material difference is there, whether the perſons addreſſing, and thoſe addreſſed, be of the ſame country, or of different countries ? The only queſtion is, whether the addreſs, or the notice, were proper or improper.

The National Aſſembly of France could not be ſo ignorant of the conſtitution of England, as to ſuppoſe that the *Revolution Society* was a body authorized by the ſtate, or that it had any connexion with the government of the country ; ſo that there could be no *fraud* or *impoſition* in the caſe ; and it may be eaſily ſuppoſed, that, being the founders of a new ſyſtem of government in France, which has hitherto been conſidered as the *natural enemy of England,*

England, they might think it wife to embrace the firſt opportunity of ſhewing that they were diſpoſed to be our *friends*, and that they took it kindly, that any number of reſpectable individuals in this country ſhould approve of their proceedings. As far as the tranſaction went, it afforded a proſpect of future good neighbourhood.

The members of the French Aſſembly would judge of the *extent* of the friendly diſpoſition of this country towards them, by the names of the perſons who promoted the meaſure ; and when they ſaw that of *Dr. Price*, ſo well known, and ſo favourably known, for true patriotiſm, diſintereſted benevolence, and public ſpirit, both in France and America, they would naturally, and juſtly, conclude, that, though no great part of the Engliſh nation was preſent, thoſe who were ſpoke the ſentiments of great numbers, and thoſe the moſt reſpectable in the country. The good will of ſuch men as Dr. Price (in whatever part of the globe, or for whatever purpoſe aſſembled) even the National Aſſembly of France might conceive to be no inconſiderable ſanction to their proceedings.

Where is the great impropriety of a nation receiving even advice, and much more accepting congratulations, from ſingle men of eminent wiſdom and virtue ? And in this light thouſands regard Dr. Price, and notwithſtanding the odium which you, in

vain,

vain, endeavour to throw upon him, and which only recoils upon yourself, his name will be known, and respected, as long as respect for religion, for virtue, and for the just rights of mankind, shall exist.

The discourse which gives you so much offence, was indeed delivered from a *pulpit*, and is commonly called a *sermon*; but this is all the impropriety that belongs to it, and therefore affects the *title* only. It was delivered to a number of political friends, on a week day, destined to a political purpose, and might perhaps as well have been delivered in the room in which the company dined. No preacher, I will venture to say, more scrupulously adapts his usual discourses to the real occasions of a christian audience, than Dr. Price does; and had you, Sir, been one of his stated hearers (though you may shudder at the idea of going into a *Conventicle*) you would, I doubt not, have been both a wiser and a better man than you now are, wise and good as you, nevertheless, may be; for I do not judge of your usual temper and disposition from the strain of this most intemperate publication. I know you, and I know it to be unworthy of you.

Besides, the pulpit has not been thought profaned by all subjects of a *political*, if of a *generally useful*, nature. If so, certainly the conduct of the clergy must be severely censured for the usual

strain

ftrain of their preaching on the 30th of January. If they preach in defence of *arbitrary power*, which they generally have done on that day, why may not we preach in defence of the great principle of *equal liberty*, and the moſt important *right of reſiſtance* to ſuch governments as they recommend?

You ſeem to take particular pleaſure in comparing *Dr. Price* to *Hugh Peters*, who expreſſed himſelf in the ſame language with reſpect to the death of king Charles, that Dr. Price has made uſe of with reſpect to the glorious proſpect of things that has opened upon us by the late Revolution in France. No doubt, a very handſome face may have ſome features reſembling thoſe in a very ugly one, and therefore Dr. Price may, without any reflexion upon him, reſemble Hugh Peters in his abhorrence of tyranny, though very different from him in other reſpects. Biſhop Burnet calls Peters "a ſort of "enthuſiaſtic buffoon preacher, and a very vitious "man," and he repreſents him as dying in the moſt cowardly manner*. But will this character apply to Dr. Price, a man whom the Preſident of the Na-

---

* Neale ſays, that after the execution of his companion Mr. Cooke, who ſuffered with the greateſt heroiſm, he reſumed his courage, and ſaid to the ſheriff, " Sir, you have ſlain one of the " ſervants of the Lord, and made me behold it, on purpoſe to ter- " rify and diſcourage me ; but God has made it an ordinance for " my ſtrengthening and encouragement."

tional Affembly of France has ftyled, and juftly
ftyled, the *Apoftle of Liberty*, though you call him
the *Doctor of Politics*, p. 17, the *Political Divine*,
p. 20, and load him with every other epithet of contempt that your exuberant imagination, unreftrained
by any regard to decency, can fupply; at the fame
time that you acknowledge, p. 13, that he has "the
"beft intentions in the world," though as an enemy
to civil eftablifhments of religion, you deny him,
p. 155, a place among *honeft enthufiafts*, and clafs
him with *cheats and deceivers*.

According to you, this Hugh Peters rode in a kind
of triumph on the bringing of king Charles a pri-
foner to London, and he may have triumphed in
an indecent and an improper manner; but, in my
opinion, there was fufficient caufe for triumph. The
thirtieth of January was (to ufe a phrafe of Admiral
Keppel's) a *proud day* for England, as well as the
fourteenth of July for France; and it will be remem-
bered as fuch by the lateft pofterity of *freemen*. Let
all tyrants read the hiftory of both, and tremble.
Good princes will read it without any unpleafant
emotion.

I am, DEAR SIR,

Yours, &c.

LETTER

L E T T E R V.

*Of the Interference of the State in Matters of Religion
in general.*

DEAR SIR,

IT was the devout wish of Job, who, with ex-
emplary patience, had borne much calumny,
as well as fufferings of other kinds, that his *adver-
fary had written a book.* The favour which this
good man could not obtain, the defpifed and oppreffed Diffenters have at length been indulged
with from you, at leaft fo far as relates to the caufe
of your ftrong attachment to the eftablifhed church
of this country, which, no doubt, induced you to
enter fo warmly as you did into the oppofition to
our late claims in the Houfe of Commons. We
are now happy in having an opportunity of view-
ing, and examining, the true fprings of your conduct, and are not obliged to collect your arguments
from uncertain report, or the mutilated, and, no
doubt, very often falfe, accounts in the newfpapers.
We have now the reafoning of the fenator from the
fenator himfelf.

E.　　　　　　　　I rather

I rather wonder, however, at this conduct in *you*, when I find you lamenting, p. 136, that " it " has been our misfortune, and not, as thefe gen- " tlemen think it" (meaning, no doubt, myfelf as well as others) " the glory of this age, that every " thing is to be *difcuffed.*" For certainly fuch a publication as this of yours, you could not but think, muft lead to much difcuffion. If, therefore, you thought this to be a dangerous procefs, with refpect either to *Church* or *State*, you certainly ought not to have entered upon it, by publifhing any thing on the fubject; unlefs, indeed, you had thought (which perhaps may have been the cafe) that your publication would effectually deter all opponents; your reafoning being fo forcible as to preclude, and be an effectual bar to, all farther dif- cuffion on the fubject; nor do I much wonder at your entertaining this idea, from the exhibition you have given us of the ftate of your own mind with refpect to it.

" Our church eftablifhment," you fay, p. 136, " is the firft of our prejudices. It is," you fay again, " the firft, the laft, and the midft in our minds," that is, it occupies the whole capacity of them, fo that they cannot admit any thing elfe, at leaft any thing of an oppofite nature. Of courfe, the maxims on which you proceed muft to *you* appear incontro- vertible. You, therefore, very naturally add, " it

" is

" is not a prejudice deſtitute of reaſon, but involving
" in it profound and extenſive wiſdom." For ſuch
is the opinion that we all entertain of prejudices
deeply rooted in our own minds; though it is no
uncommon thing for what appears to be *profound
and extenſive wiſdom* to one man, to appear the extreme of *folly* to another ; and unfortunately (owing
perhaps to the difference of our educations, and
early habits) this is preciſely the difference between
you and me. What you admire I deſpiſe, and what
you think highly uſeful, I am perſuaded is very miſ-
chievous.

However, notwithſtanding the great difference
in our *concluſions*, we have, I perceive, ſome great
and leading *common principles* ; ſo that it may not be
difficult to diſcover which of us has departed the
fartheſt from them. I ſhall endeavour to ſhew our
readers, that with theſe common principles, your
concluſions are wholly diſcordant ; and I flatter my-
ſelf that, differently as we think on a variety of
ſubjects, we have more common principles than
you have given ſufficient attention to, and more
than you really act upon. You cannot, for example, have that diſlike to *diſcuſſion* which you profeſs,
becauſe, in this and in other publications, as well
as in your ſpeeches in the Houſe of Commons, you
have entered largely into many diſcuſſions ; and you
muſt alſo agree with me in thinking, that the more

E 2   important

important any fubject is, or the more interefting it is to men, either as individuals, or members of fo-ciety, the greater call there is for an accurate dif-cuffion of every thing relating to it; becaufe, in things of this nature, miftakes are the moft dan-gerous, and you are far from fuppofing *religion* to be a matter of indifference, either to individuals, or to fociety. And how can we guard againft, or indeed be apprized of, any miftakes, without due examination, or difcuffion?

That our readers may fee at one view what it is that you maintain with refpect to civil eftablifh-ments of religion, I fhall, before I enter upon the difcuffion of them, give our readers a fummary view of all your pofitions. Confounding, as you evidently do, the idea of *religion* itfelf, with that of the *civil eftablifhment* of it, you fay, "It is the "bafis of civil fociety, and effential to every ftate," infomuch that you even queftion whether it be *lawful* to be without one. So far, you think, is the church from having any dependence upon the ftate, that the ftate has not even "the property, or do-"minion," of any thing belonging to the church, being only the "guardian" of the revenues of the church, and holding them in truft for its ufe. You, therefore, hold that the property of the church is unalienable, and not to be touched in any emer-gency of ftate whatever. Religion, you maintain,
derives

derives its estimation and effect, from the riches and magnificence of its establishment; that such establishment is calculated for the multitude, that it is peculiarly useful both to the poor and the rich, and, though necessary to all states, is more proper for a democratical, than any other form of government.

Now, Sir, strange as it may appear to you, my ideas, in all these respects, are the very reverse of yours. Religion I consider as a thing that requires no civil establishment whatever, and that its beneficial operation is injured by such establishment, and the more in proportion to its riches. I am satisfied that such an establishment, instead of being any advantage, is a great incumbrance to a state, and in general highly unfavourable to its liberties. Civil establishments of christianity were altogether unknown in the early ages, and gained ground by very slow degrees, as other corruptions and abuses in the system did. I am clearly of opinion, that the state has a right to dispose of all property within itself; that of the church, as well as of every thing else of a public nature, and that religion has naturally nothing at all to do with any particular form of civil government; being useful indeed to all persons, the rich as well as the poor, but only as individuals.

E 3

Let

Let us now trace our very different ideas to their proper fource, and compare them with our common principles ; and I am happy to find that we agree with refpect to the proper ufe and advantage of government in general, which is a very material circumſtance in our difcuſſion. " Government, " you fay, p. 88, is a contrivance of human wif- " dom, to provide for human wants, and men have " a right that thefe wants be provided for by this " wifdom."

You will not, however, fay that *all* human wants are to be provided for by government ; for it is manifeſtly only *fome* of them that its great power can reach, and therefore much muſt be left to the individuals themſelves. This you allow, when you fay, p. 87, " whatever each man can feparately " do, without trefpaſſing upon others, he has a right " to do for himſelf." Since then I can *eat* and *drink* whatever fuits my appetite, without trefpaſſing upon any body, you will allow that the ſtate has no bufineſs to prefcribe what I ſhall eat or drink, or when, or in what manner, I ſhall do it. I imagine, alfo, you will allow that my neighbours have no right to complain of me, if, when I am indif-pofed, I treat myfelf as I think proper, taking whatever advice, or whatever medicines, I pleafe. They may do the fame, and I ſhall not complain

of

of them. Pray then, what right, on this plain and obvious principle, advanced by yourſelf, has any man to complain of me if I *worſhip God* in what manner I pleaſe, or if I do not chuſe to worſhip God at all? Does my conduct in this reſpect injure them? What, then, has the ſtate, or my neighbours, to do in this buſineſs, any more than with my food or my medicine?

In this, and many other things, government has taken a great deal too much upon it; and has by this means brought itſelf into great and needleſs embarraſſments. In many things beſides the article of religion, men have buſied themſelves in *legiſlating* too much, and when it would have been better if individuals had been left to think and act for themſelves.

This, you will ſay, amounts to nothing more than a plea for *toleration* in matters of religion, which you are ready to allow. As a foundation for a *civil eſtabliſhment* of religion, you ſay that " man " is by his conſtitution a religious animal;" for all that follows in defence of eſtabliſhments, is immediately connected with *this*. Now, admitting this, which however is not true (becauſe we may eaſily conceive of a Being, poſſeſſed of all the eſſential properties of *human nature*, without any knowledge of religion at all) government can have no more right to interfere with reſpect to *this* conſtitutional

E 4 property

property of man, than any other conftitutional, or effential property ; and with refpect to many of thefe, you muft allow that men fhould be left to themfelves.   For example, man is conftitutionally and neceffarily an *eating* and a *fleeping* animal; but does it therefore follow that civil government has any thing to do with his eating or fleeping ? And if not, neither has it any right to prefcribe to him in matters of *religion*, merely becaufe he is by confti-tution a *religious animal*.   Man is a *thinking* and *rea-foning* animal ; but muft all his thinking and rea-foning be fubject to the control of the ftate ? Man has alfo been defined to be *animal rifibile*, but muft we therefore never laugh but when our grave and wife governors fhall give us leave ? We often indulge ourfelves even in laughing at them.

As you do not deal much in *definitions*, or *axioms*, I am obliged to collect your idea of the *principle* on which church eftablifhments are founded, from cafual expreffions, and the general fcope of your declamation.   Syftematical divines, in this country, have, in different circumftances of their affairs, advanced two very different principles, as the bafis of civil eftablifhments of religion.   At firft it was univerfally afferted that chriftianity, and fome par-ticular form of it, ought to be eftablifhed, main-tained, and protected, by the civil power, becaufe it was *true*; that it became the civil magiftrate, as

the

the *vicegerent of God*, to ftand up for the honour of God, and of his truth ; fo that it was of no confequence at all what was the religion of his fub-jects. It was his duty to inforce *truth*, and to bring them as foon as he could to the profeffion and due maintenance of it.

But when it was urged that civil magiftrates were not always the beft judges of religious truth, that they had often little leifure for the ftudy of re-ligion, and were apt to be impofed upon by priefts, and others whofe intereft it was to miflead them; befides that, upon this plan, the religion of every coun-try, would be liable to be changed with every change of governors, as was the cafe in our own country, in feveral fucceffive reigns after that of Henry VIII. or rather Henry VII. this old ground was fhifted; and of late it has been maintained by our high church divines, and by yourfelf, who muft be claffed with them, that the civil magiftrate has no-thing to do with the *truth* of religion, being obliged to provide for that which is profeffed by the *majority* of the fubjects, though he himfelf fhould be of a different perfuafion. Thus they fay the king of Great Britain, muft maintain epifcopacy in England, and prefbyterianifm in Scotland, whether he be a prefby-terian as king William, a Lutheran as George I. or a true churchman as his prefent Majefty.

You,

You, Sir, appear to defend church eſtabliſhments on the latter of theſe principles. "The chriſtian "ſtateſman," you ſay, p. 151, "muſt firſt provide "for the multitude, becauſe it is the multitude, and "is therefore, as ſuch, the firſt object in the eccle- "ſiaſtical inſtitution, and in all inſtitutions." But how does this apply to the caſe of your country of Ireland. For the very ſame reaſon that epiſ- copacy ought to be eſtabliſhed in England, and preſbyterianiſm in Scotland, the Roman catholic ought to be the eſtabliſhed religion of Ireland, be- cauſe, as I apprehend, it is unqueſtionably the re- ligion of a very great majority of the inhabitants. As to the great maſs of the oppreſſed Iriſh, if they be aſked whether it be *their* religion, that which they really approve, that they are obliged to main- tain, they will ſay it is a *foreign* one, one that they diſbelieve and deteſt, and yet are compelled to ſup- port, whilſt from genuine zeal, they think it their duty to maintain their own. It is not ſuppoſed that more than one in ten of the inhabitants of Ireland are of the church of England, and yet the iron hand of power compels them to maintain it. Is this, think you, the way to recommend your reli- gion? Judge by the effect. What converts have been made to it in the laſt two centuries? The zealous members of your church, in the reign of

the

the two Charles's of blefsed memory, impofed epifcopacy alfo upon Scotland, when not more than
one in a hundred of the Scots would attend the
fervice; but the generous fpirit of that nation at
length threw off the oppreffive yoke. The Irifh
alfo have the will, but, alas, not the power.

If you will have an eftablifhment, and act upon
the principles that you profefs, viz. to provide for
the *multitude*, or the great mafs of the people, do
you, of your own accord, change the eftablifhed religion of Ireland, to one more confonant to the ge-
nius and wifhes of the nation; and let it not be faid
that the church of England would have the impu-
dence, if it had the power, to collect its tithes from
every country in chriftendom, though every parifh
fhould be a *finecure,* and all their bifhops be denominated *in partibus.* Let there be an appearance at
leaft, which now there is not, of fome regard to
religion in the cafe, and not to mere *revenue.* Often as I have urged this fubject, and many as have
been thofe who have animadverted upon my writings, hardly any have touched upon *this.* They feel it
to be tender ground. They can, however, keep an
obftinate filence, they can fhut their ears, and turn
their eyes to other objects, when it is not to their
purpofe to attend to this.

Admitting that religion muft be *eftablifhed,* or
fupported by civil power, in order to its efficiency,

will

will *any* ſpecies of religion anſwer the purpoſe; the heathen, or the Mahometan, as well as the chriſtian, and one ſpecies of chriſtianity as well as another? Muſt we have no *diſcuſſion* concerning the nature, and influence, of the different kinds of religion, in order that, if we happen to have got a worſe, we may relieve ourſelves by ſubſtituting a better in its place? Muſt every thing once eſtabliſhed be, for that reaſon only, ever maintained? This is ſaid, indeed, to be your maxim, openly avowed in the Houſe of Commons, and, it is perfectly agreeable to every thing advanced in this publication. For you condemn the French National Aſſembly, for innovating in *their* religion, which is Catholic, as much as you could do the Engliſh Parliament, for innovating in *ours*, which is Proteſtant. You condemn them for lowering the ſtate of archbiſhops, biſhops, and abbots, though they have improved that of the lower orders of the clergy; and therefore you would, no doubt, be equally offended at any diminution of the power of cardinals, or of the pope. We may therefore preſume, that had you lived in Turkey, you would have been a mahometan, and in Tartary, a devout worſhipper of the grand lama.

It is amuſing to ſee with what confidence, and with what various expreſſion, you deliver your ſentiments on the ſubject of theſe civil eſtabliſhments of religion, without diſtinguiſhing one from another.

other. " This principle," you say. p. 147, " runs
" through the whole system of their" (the British)
" policy. They do not consider their church
" establishment as convenient, but as essential to
" their state, not as a thing heterogeneous and se-
" parable, something added for accommodation,
" what they may either keep at or lay aside, ac-
" cording to their temporary ideas of convenience.
" They consider it as the foundation of their whole
" constitution, with which, and with every part
" of which, it holds an indissoluble union. *Church*
" and *state* are ideas inseparable in their minds, and
" scarcely is the one ever mentioned, without men-
" tioning the other. It is on such principles,"
you say, " that the majority of the people of Eng-
" land, far from thinking a religious national esta-
" blishment unlawful, hardly think it lawful to be
" without one. In France you are wholly mis-
" taken if you do not believe us above all other
" things attached to it, and above all other na-
" tions."

Now you cannot be so little read in the history
of England, as not to know that the *church* and
state were as much connected before the Reformation as they have been since, and while the establishment was presbyterian, as well as now that it is epis-
copalian. You must know also that the inhabitants
of this country, were at one time as zealous papists

as they now are proteftants, and yet they were brought to make a change in their eftablifhed re-ligion, and that this was done without making any material change in the fyftem of civil government. You muft know that the prefbyterians in Scotland, and the epifcopalians in England, have at this very time the fame king and the fame parliament. But how do thefe facts agree with your favourite idea of the infeparable union of church and ftate? What, then, is the foundation of the dread you have en-tertained of any *future* change in the religion of our country, when no harm, but, as all proteftants think, much advantage, has been derived from *paft* changes in it?

I am, DEAR SIR,

Yours, &c.

LETTER

LETTER VI.

Of the Source of the Respect that is paid to Religion.

DEAR SIR,

THAT you make no difference between chriftianity and the civil eftablifhment of it, is evident from many parts of your performance, and that you confider the *refpect* which it commands, as intirely derived from the circumftances of its eftablifhment, is equally evident. After reprefenting the importance of chriftianity, as oppofed to infidelity, you fay, in a peculiar ftrain of eloquence, p. 135, " If in the moment of riot, and in a drunken
" delirium, from the hot fpirit drawn out of the
" alembic of hell, which in France is now fo fu-
" rioufly boiling, we fhould uncover our naked-
" nefs, by throwing off that chriftian religion,
" which has hitherto been our boaft and comfort,
" and one great fource of civilization among us,
" and among many other nations, we are appre-
" henfive (being well aware that the mind will not
" endure a void) that fome uncouth, pernicious,
" and

" and degrading fuperftition might take place of it.
" For that reafon, before we take from our efta-
" blifhment the *natural human means of eftimation,*
" and give it up to contempt, as you have done
" (and in doing it have incurred the penalties you
" well deferve to fuffer) we defire that fome other
" may be prefented to us in the place of it. We
" fhall then form our judgment. On thefe ideas,
" inftead of quarrelling with eftablifhments, as fome
" do who have made a philofophy, and a religion, of
" their hoftility to fuch inftitutions, we cleave clofely
" to them. We are refolved to keep an efta-
" blifhed church, an eftablifhed monarchy, an
" eftablifhed ariftocracy, and an eftablifhed demo-
" cracy, each in the degree it exifts, and in no
" greater."

It is evident from this paffage (the whole of which
is fo fublimely rhetorical, that I could not help tranf-
cribing it, though not abfolutely neceffary to my
purpofe) that you confider the chriftian religion as
having no *refpectability,* or *effect,* without being
eftablifhed, and that the *natural human means of the*
eftimation in which it is held, is the fplendour and
riches of fuch an eftablifhment ; and this will be ftill
more evident from fome paffages that I fhall have
occafion to quote hereafter. Let us now confider
how this idea accords with the *principles* of chriftianity, and the authentic *records* of it, which you

" will

will allow to be contained in the books of the New Teſtament, and alſo with its well known ſubſequent *biſtory*.

Did our Saviour give his apoſtles any inſtructions about connecting his religion with civil power, as if it would ever ſtand in need of ſuch aid; or did the apoſtles, more fully inſtructed after his death and aſcenſion, give any intimation of this kind? On the contrary, our Saviour declared that *his kingdom was not of this world*, which muſt mean that it did not reſemble other kingdoms, in being ſupported by public taxes, and having its laws guarded by civil penalties. The apoſtles, and all chriſtian miniſters, for many centuries, lived on the voluntary contributions of their reſpective churches, and they had no means of enforcing their cenſures beſides excluſion from their ſocieties; and can you ſay that chriſtianity wanted any proper *eſtimation*, or *reſpectability*, in that period? Did it not abundantly recommend itſelf to every attentive candid obſerver, and to every impartial inquirer; and did it not by this means continually gain ground, notwithſtanding it was oppoſed both by all the temporal powers of the world, and by whatever was moſt ſplendid and faſcinating in the eſtabliſhed ſyſtems of heathenifm? It was the *virtue*, it was the well known piety and extenſive benevolence, of the primitive chriſtians, and ˏnot wealth or power, that procured

F   reſpect

respect to themselves, and to their cause. Read only the letters of the Emperor Julian, and you cannot but be sensible of this. To this, and to this alone, *he* ascribed the respect that was then paid to christianity, and the progress it had made in the world.

If you suppose, as you really seem to do, that christianity is now destitute of these proper *means of estimation*, you know little of its nature or power. The *truths* and the *promises* of the gospel are the same now that they ever were, nor is its *evidence* at all diminished; and *human nature*, on which it operates, you will not doubt, is also the same. And if you could look at any thing out of an establishment, you might see that christianity even now produces as disinterested and heroic virtue as ever it did. It forms men alike for the most active usefulness, or the most patient suffering. But amusing yourself with the *shadow* you wholly neglect the *substance*. Looking at *religion*, you see nothing but the civil establishments of it. Thus have I sometimes seen an aged *oak* so completely covered with a luxuriant *ivy*, that it required some attention to discern any thing else.

That wealth and splendour have not the charms that you ascribe to them with the bulk of mankind, is evident even from the history of *Monachism*, one of the corruptions of christianity. The first monks were not attracted by magnificent monasteries, and highly ornamented churches, but were most numerous, when they had nothing but the deserts to retire to. Then also were they the most respected; and they did not sink into contempt till they had acquired what you call the *natural human means of estimation.* The same has been the case with the secular clergy, in all countries. They were infinitely more respected, even by the rich and the great, while they were poor, than they have ever been since they have got their present splendid establishments; nor is it difficult to see the cause of this, and how it operates. Ease, affluence, and power, attract persons who have no sense or knowledge of religion; and when mere *men of the world* get ecclesiastical preferment, they will, of course, disgrace their profession by their vices. It was the unbounded luxury, profligacy, and arrogance, of the court of Rome, possessed as you think of every natural human means of estimation, that was one of the principal causes of the reformation.

According to your maxims, a rich establishment should make its clergy more respected then a poor one. But does this appear to be the case, on the comparison of the state of the clergy in Scotland, and those in this country? Dr. Adam Smith, who well knew them both, was of a very different opinion; and the most superficial observer must be

F 2

sen-

senfible that he is in the right. Nay, so unfortunate is the situation of the clergy in this country (for it cannot be any thing, but their *situation*, *men* being the same in all countries) that, by the confession of many persons in the establishment itself, there are no clergy in christendom more negligent of their proper duty, less strict in their morals, and consequently *more despised*, than they are. Bishop Burnet, who had been much abroad, and who was an attentive observer, was decidedly of this opinion; and the character of the clergy in general, is little, if it all, improved since his time.

The manner in which your imagination is struck with a splendid church establishment, makes you even exceed yourself in *eloquence*; and, as I always admire you in this field, though not in that of sober *reasoning*, I cannot forbear quoting a pretty long paragraph to this purpose, as it is particularly excellent in its kind. " He," you say, p. 146, " who gave our " nature to be perfected by our virtue, willed also " the necessary means of its perfection. He willed " therefore the state. He willed its connection with " the source and original archetype of all perfec- " tion" (meaning, no doubt, *the church*, equally the archetype of all perfection in Indostan, in Turkey, in Italy, in England, and even in Scotland) " They who are convinced of this his will, " which is the law of laws, and the sovereign of

" sovereigns,

" sovereigns, cannot think it reprehensible that this
" our corporate fealty and homage, that this our
" recognition of a signiory paramount, I had almost
" said this oblation of the state itself, as a worthy
" offering on the high altar of universal praise,
" should be performed, as all public solemn acts are
" performed, in buildings, in music, in decoration,
" in speech, in the dignity of persons, according to
" the customs of mankind, taught by their nature;
" that is, with modest splendour, with unassuming
" state, with mild majesty, and sober pomp. For
" those purposes they think some part of the wealth
" of the country is as usefully employed as it can
" be in fomenting the luxury of individuals. It is
" the public consolation. It nourishes the public
" hope. The poorest man finds his own impor-
" tance and dignity in it, whilst the wealth and
" pride of individuals at every moment makes the
" man of humble rank and fortune sensible of his
" inferiority, and degrades and vilifies his condition.
" It is for the man in humble life, and to raise his
" nature, and to put him in mind of a state in which
" the privileges of opulence will cease, when he will
" be equal by nature, and may be more than equal
" by virtue, that this portion of the general wealth
" of his country is employed and sanctified."

Big with these ideas, you say, p. 153, " as the
" mass of any description of men are but men, and

F 3 " their

" their poverty" (namely that of the clergy) " can-
" not be voluntary, that difrespect which attends
" upon all lay-poverty will not depart from the
" ecclefiaftical.   Our conftitution has therefore
" taken care, that thofe who are to inftruct prefump-
" tuous ignorance, thofe who are to be cenfors over
" infolent vice, fhould neither incur their contempt,
" nor live upon their alms; nor will it tempt the
" rich to a neglect of the true medicine of their
" minds.   For thefe reafons, while we provide firft
" for the poor, with a parental folicitude, we have
" not relegated religion, like fomething we were
" afhamed to fhew, to obfcure municipalities, or
" ruftic villages.   No ; we will have her to exalt
" her mitred front in courts and parliaments.   We
" will have her mixed throughout the whole mafs
" of life, and blended with all the claffes of fo-
" ciety.   The people of England will fhew to the
" haughty potentates of the world, and to their
" talking fophifters, that a free, a generous, and in-
" formed nation, honours the high magiftrates of
" its church, that it will not fuffer the infolence
" of wealth and titles, or any other fpecies of proud
" pretenfion, to look down with fcorn upon what
" they look up to with reverence, nor prefume to
" trample on that acquired perfonal nobility which
" they intend always to be, and which often is, the
" fruit, not the reward (for what can be the re-
                                        " ward)

" ward) of learning, piety, and virtue. They can
" fee without pain or grudging an archbifhop pre-
" cede a duke. They can fee a bifhop of Dur-
" ham, or a bifhop of Winchefter, in poffeffion of
" ten thoufand pounds a year," &c. &c. &c.

Pray, Sir, on what part of the New Teftament is
this a comment? Alas, it is the *wifdom of the world*,
which *is foolifhnefs with God*, and even with ferious
and fenfible men? The wealth of the clergy, of
which you are fo proud, and the temporal power
with which you have invefted them, is the natural
fource of their corruption, and what muft ever fink
them, and religion, into contempt. Has the fplendour of the ecclefiaftical eftablifhment in France,
which is much fuperior to any thing of the kind
in this country, prevented the fpread of the Reformation on the one hand, or of infidelity on the
other? By your own account, France is almoft a
nation of infidels, at leaft their National Affembly,
in your idea, confifts chiefly of them. Have the
remains of this fplendour, refpectable ftill in your
eyes, prevented the rejection of chriftianity altogether *here?* If you know the world, and even
what paffes at home, you muft know the contrary.
Infidelity has made confiderable progrefs in this
country, and efpecially in the upper claffes of life,
perfons to whom you imagine the wealth of the clergy
would naturally recommend their religion. But

F 4

their

thefe men do not frequent your churches, and they regard your eftablifhment no farther than they can avail themfelves of its emoluments, as it is a means of providing for their younger fons and brothers. If the Houfes of Lords and Commons were fairly polled, after voting according to their *real opinion*, whether, think you, would the majority be in favour of chriftianity, or againft it? Many, and thofe not inattentive obfervers, think the latter.

If riches and power have the charms which you afcribe to them in the bufinefs of religion, how came the *reformation* to take place? The power and fplendour of the church of Rome was at its height in the time of Luther and his followers; yet, without any aid of this kind to oppofe to it, in Germany, in this country, or in Scotland, it gave way to the efforts of men who had no advantage but what they derived from reafon and piety. Surely, Sir, the bulk of mankind do not fee with your eyes. If they did, how can you account for the great number of Diffenters in this country, from the time of Queen Elizabeth, who had the fame ideas that you have on thefe fubjects, down to the prefent time; and what can be the caufe of the amazing increafe of methodifm? Neither their minifters nor ours are rich. We have not the ftyle of *my lord*, nor have we feats in parliament. But, deftitute as we are of all thefe advantages, I will venture to

say,

ſay, that our miniſters, as a body, are much more reſpected by their congregations than yours, poſ-ſeſſed, in your idea, of all the *natural human means of eſtimation.*

Judging of us by yourſelves, you naturally ſup-poſe, that it is only through *envy* and *malignity*, that we declaim againſt the wealth and the power of the clergy. " In England, you ſay, p. 155, " moſt " of us conceive that it is envy and malignity to-" wards thoſe who are often the beginners of their " own fortune, and not a love of the ſelf-denial " and mortification of the ancient church, that makes " ſome look aſkance at the diſtinctions, and honours, " and revenues, which, taken from no perſon, are " ſet apart for virtue. The ears of the people of " England are diſtinguiſhing. They hear theſe " men ſpeak broad. Their tongue betrays them. " Their language is in the *patois* of fraud, in the " cant and gibberiſh of hypocriſy. The people of " England muſt think ſo when theſe praters affect " to carry back the clergy to that primitive evan-" gelic poverty, which, in the ſpirit, ought always " to exiſt in *them* (and in *us* too, however, we may " like it) but the thing muſt be varied, when the " the relation of that body to the ſtate is altered, " when manners, when modes of life, when indeed " the whole order of human affairs, has undergone " a total revolution. We ſhall believe theſe re-" formers

" formers to be then *honest enthusiasts*, not, as now
" we think them, *cheats* and *deceivers*, when we see
" them throwing their own goods into common,
" and submitting their own persons to the austere
" discipline of the early church."

This, Sir, is a paragraph of which it is to be hoped you will some time hence be ashamed. You do not give us the alternative of being either *knaves* or *fools*. You will not allow us any place in this more respectable, or rather less contemptible, class of men. None of us who disapprove of establishments, Dr. Price, or myself, can have the honour of being ranked with *honest enthusiasts*. We are all absolutely, and without a single exception, *cheats* and *deceivers*, who are saying one thing, and, at the same time, meaning another. But we are happy in an appeal from your judgment, as you are from ours; though, judging from myself, we are by no means disposed to censure you with so much severity as you do us. I do not say that we are so mortified to the world, as that the good things with which you tempt us, have no charms for us. We are *men*, and have the feelings of men, as well as yourselves. But if they struck our imagination as forcibly as they do yours, and if we were the *knaves* and *hypocrites* that you suppose us to be, why do we not make greater efforts to obtain them? The market is open, but we do not chuse to give the price.

price. If thefe things be acceffible to *fome*, they are no doubt to *others*, in proportion to their ability or intereft, or whatever it be that affifts their preferment.

As to fubfcription to your articles, &c. if I be fuch a perfon as you have defcribed, why might not I declare my *unfeigned affent and confent* to them, as well as others? Befides, if the advantages of an eftablifhment were the things that we are aiming at, why are we labouring at the fubverfion of *all* eftablifhments, expofing their inutility, and even their mifchievous nature and tendency? If the tree be cut down, how are we to live upon the fruit of it? And there are now, I believe, very few Diffenters, who, if the prefent eftablifhment was overturned, would wifh to fubftitute any other in its place.

Your idea of the ftate of things in the primitive church, is altogether founded on miftake. It was not, from the firft, materially different from what it is, or at leaft ought to be, at this day, and therefore did not require any great difference in the condition of its ordinary minifters. There never was any obligation on chriftians to *throw their goods into common*. Whatever was done of this kind, appears from the hiftory of Ananias and Sapphira, to have been perfectly voluntary, and could not have been univerfal; and we read of no fuch things

in

in any of the Gentile churches. Thefe, from the firft, confifted of *rich* and *poor*, and the rich among them made contributions to relieve the poor chriftians at Jerufalem, which could not have been wanted, if all the rich, even there, had given their all. As to the *difcipline* of the primitive church, it was fuch as I fhould have no objection to, but have ftrongly recommended in my *Effay on Church Difcipline*; nor was it more ftrict than is actually exercifed in feveral chriftian churches, though not in that of England, at this day. But of thefe things you, Sir, feem to fpeak altogether at random, without any particular knowledge of the fubject.

I am, Dear Sir,

Yours, &c.

LETTER VII.

Of a civil Eſtabliſhment being eſſential to Chriſtianity.

DEAR SIR,

IF a civil eſtabliſhment be ſo eſſential as you re-
preſent it, to the eſtimation and effect of chriſtianity, you muſt, no doubt, imagine that it never
exiſted without one, that it has *grown with its
growth, and ſtrengthened with its ſtrength.* Hence
your apprehenſion that, if any thing affect the
one, it muſt in proportion affect the other, and
that they muſt both ſtand or fall together. Now,
being yourſelf nothing more than a *lay divine* (as
you contemptuouſly characteriſe a perſon of emi-
nence, who has preſumed to *hint* at ſome improve-
ments in your favourite ſyſtem, not calculated to
overturn, but to ſtrengthen it) I, whom, together
with Dr. Price, you will claſs, p. 13, among *political theologians,* and *theological politicians,* ſhall give
you a little information on the ſubject. Your talents, no doubt, are great ; but what are talents,
or powers of reaſoning, and combining particular

ſacts

facts into fyftems, if a man have no facts to combine, no proper knowledge of his fubject? In this
cafe his greater ingenuity will only ferve to miflead him, and fix him in error. And it is very
evident that, whatever has been the compafs of
your ftudies, *ecclefiaftical hiftory* has not been within
its range ; and facts, notorious facts, fuch as lye upon the very face and furface of it, unfortunately
overturn your whole fyftem.

You have not been pleafed to give us the defini-
tion of an *eftablifhed church*, though you enlarge fo
much in your encomiums upon it ; but in this
we cannot much difagree. In its full extent, it is
a church defended, and even regulated, by the ftate,
which either wholly profcribes, tolerates, or barely
connives at, other religions. Now, what was the
fituation of the chriftian church with refpect to the
State in the primitive times ? You muft know that,
fo far from being fupported by the civil powers
(which were then either Jewifh or Heathen) it was
frowned upon by them, and violently perfecuted, itfelf
being at that time nothing more than a *fect*, or a
herefy, fometimes connived at, but never openly
tolerated ; and yet in thefe circumftances it exifted,
and flourifhed, gradually gaining ground by its own
evidence, till it triumphed over all oppofition, and
the Roman empire itfelf became chriftian.

What

What was it thefe chriftian emperors then did for their religion? They did little or nothing towards its *fupport*, becaufe they found it fufficiently fupported by the voluntary contributions and benefactions of its friends. They did, however, *what they ought not to have done*; they influenced the decifions of councils, and enforced them by temporal pains and penalties. The State alfo protected property given or bequeathed to the church, as well as that which was appropriated to other ufes; but there was nothing like a *tax* levied for the fupport of religion for many ages, nor is there any fuch thing at this day in a very great part of the chriftian world. Tithes are comparatively but a modern invention, the payment of them being firft voluntary, and afterwards obligatory; and the compulfory payment of tithes did not take place in the whole of this country till the time of King John, of *glorious and immortal memory*, on that account. There are now no tithes paid in the ecclefiaftical ftates of Italy, or in Sicily, and though, as I have been lately informed, there is what is called tithes in fome parts of Lombardy, it does not in general exceed one thirtieth part of the produce, and is never one tenth.

Another important article in *our* ecclefiaftical eftablifhment, is the right of our kings to the no

mination of bifhops *. But it is well known, that
the right of chufing the bifhops was originally, and
for many centuries, in their refpective churches,
the metropolitans fhewing their approbation by
joining in their ordination; and that even the emperors themfelves, after they became chriftians,
never affumed any fuch authority. It was firft
ufurped by the popes, in the plenitude of their
power, and by the feudal princes of Europe, in
confequence of their invefting bifhops with their
temporalities, and making them *lerds of territory*.
The National Affembly of France have, to their
immortal honour (though they fhould be diffolved
to-morrow, and never meet again) reftored to all
the chriftian churches in that country, their original right of appointing their own paftors, both
the ordinary clergy and the bifhops.

As to the claim of our princes to be the *heads
of the church* (which is an ufurpation from an ufur-
per, the pope) and that of our parliament, to
enact what fhall be deemed *articles of faith*, and
to give a form and conftitution to the whole
church, it is a thing not fo much as pretended to

* This is done in England by the king iffuing a *Conge d'Elire* to
the chapters of each cathedral, impowering them to chufe fuch
perfons only as are named to them; but in Ireland it is done without this form.

by

by any other temporal power in the world, and a greater abfurdity and abufe than any thing fubfifting in the fyftem of popery, where at leaft the judges in ecclefiaftical affairs are ecclefiaftical perfons.

The whole fyftem of the civil eftablifhment of religion had its origin at a time when neither *religion* nor *civil government* was much underftood. It was the confequence of the feudal ftates of Europe becoming chriftian in an age where we find little of Chriftianity, befides the *name*; its genuine *doctrines* and its *fpirit* having equally difappeared.

Every article, therefore, within the compafs of the civil eftablifhment of chriftianity, is evidently an *innovation*; and as fyftems are reformed by reverting to their firft principles, chriftianity can never be reftored to its priftine ftate, and recover its real dignity and efficiency, till it be difengaged from all connexion with civil power. This eftablifhment, therefore, may be compared to a *fungus*, or a *parafitical plant*, which is fo far from being coeval with the tree on which it has faftened itfelf, that it feized upon it in its weak and languid ftate, and if it be not cut off in time, will exhauft all its juices, and deftroy it.

Writing to an orator, I naturally think of metaphors and comparifons, and therefore I will give you two or three more. So far is a civil eftablifhment from being friendly to chriftianity, that it may be com-

pared

pared to the animal, called the *Sloth*, which, when it gets upon any tree, will not leave it till it has devoured even the leaves and the bark, so that it presently perishes. Rather, it is the animal called a *glutton*, which falling from a tree (in which it generally conceals itself) upon some noble animal, immediately begins to tear it, and suck its blood; and if it be not soon shaken off (which sometimes every effort fails to effect) it infallibly kills its prey.

Now, when I see this *fungus* of an establishment upon the noble plant of christianity, draining its best juices; when I see this *Sloth* upon its stately branches, gnawing it, and stripping it bare; or, to change my comparison, when I see the *Glutton* upon the shoulders of this noble animal, the blood flowing down, and its very vitals in danger; if I wish to preserve the tree, or the animal, must I not, without delay, extirpate the fungus, destroy the Sloth, and kill the Glutton. Indeed, Sir, say, or write, what you please, such vermin deserve no mercy. You may stand by, and weep for the fate of your favourite fungus, your Sloth, or your Glutton, but I shall not spare them.

In your idea, a civil establishment is the very *less*, or *foundation* of religion. But when any structure is to be raised, the foundation is the first thing that is laid; whereas this was evidently the very last. Instead, therefore, of its being the *foundation*, or even the *buttreſs*, it may rather be ſaid to reſemble the heavy *ſtone roof*, preſſing with an enormous weight upon the walls, which on that account require many buttreſſes to ſupport it, and after all proves to be ſo heavy, and is now become ſo ruinous, that it will be found abſolutely neceſſary to take it all down, if the building is to be preſerved. Nay, as in the late taking down of the ſtone roof of the cathedral, I think, of Hereford, if the greateſt care be not taken, the attempt to meddle with this cumbrous roof will be hazardous, both to thoſe who remove it, and thoſe who ſtand near it.

I am, DEAR SIR,

Yours, &c.

LETTER VIII.

Of the Uses of civil Establishments of Religion.

DEAR SIR,

YOU certainly magnify the benefits derived from religion itself too much, valuable as I allow it to be, when you say, p. 134, " We know, and " what is better, we feel, that religion is the basis " of civil society, and the source of all good and of " all comfort." Here, surely, is more of the *rhetori- cian* than of the *reasoner*, even supposing you not to mean, what you evidently do, the civil establish- ment of religion, but religion itself. Is there no good, or comfort, in any thing but religion, or what flows from it ? Will religion feed or cloath us ; or is there no comfort in food or cloathing ? Is it not possible to make many wholesome laws to prevent men from injuring one another, and is it not possible to execute those laws, so as to preserve the *peace of society*, which I conceive to be the pro- per end of civil government, without calling in the aid of religion ; or cannot religion operate in aid of good laws, without the help of the magistrate ?

Civil

Civil eſtabliſhments of religion, muſt, however, be imagined to be of *ſome uſe* to ſociety, or it will be of little conſequence to defend them at all. If the church, or the king, have nothing but *divine right* to ſtand upon, the people, ſeeing their own in-tereſt to be of the queſtion, would not, at this day, ſhew much zeal in their ſupport. They muſt, if poſſible, be made to believe, that a ſyſtem ſupport-ed by their money, and the ſweat of their brows, is, in ſome way or other, directly or indirectly, for their advantage. Accordingly, you, Sir, have found it neceſſary to urge the *utility* of theſe eſtabliſhments, and according to you, this utility is threefold. They are of uſe to the poor, and to the rich, and though they ſuit all governments, they are more par-ticularly neceſſary in democratical ones.

"The chriſtian ſtateſmen," you ſay, p. 151, " of " this land have been taught, that the circumſtance " of the goſpel's being preached to the poor, was " one of the great teſts of its true miſſion. They " think, therefore, that thoſe do not believe it who " do not take care it ſhould be preached to the " poor."

Here, Sir, your argument, as far as there is any thing of argument in it, is, that ſince the poor cannot afford to pay for religious inſtruction, the ſtate ſhould provide it for them. A very pious and charitable deſign, no doubt; but at whoſe expence

G 3

is this provifion made ? If it were at the expence of
the rich only, there would be fomething of charity
in it ; but is not all property, that of the poor as
well as that of the rich, taxed alike for this purpofe ?
Do not the clergy exact the payment of *fmall tithes*,
and often with the utmoft rigour, from their pooreft parifhioners ? Do we not fometimes hear of
their being actually turned out of their little tene-
ments, by a diftrefs levied by their fpiritual inftruc-
tors; and are not the poor Irifh, fome of the moft deftitute and miferable of mankind, driven into almoft annual rebellions, by oppreffion from the ex-
action of tithes ?

This, I am told, is the true caufe of the rife of
thofe who are called *White Boys,* among the poor
catholics of Ireland ; and nothing but the terror of
military execution, can compel them to pay for
that inftruction which you would give us to underftand is fo charitably afforded them. Thus, to be
compelled to pay for the inftruction which they deteft,
and receive no advantage from, and to be at the
fame time under another kind of neceffity of paying
for the inftruction which they really value, is, indeed, a hard cafe. But this, according to you, is
preaching the gofpel to the poor.

The gofpel was, in its proper fenfe, preached to
the poor by our Saviour, the apoftles, and other
primitive chriftians, who were themfelves poor.

In

In thofe times, all the contributions for the maintenance of public worfhip, were made by the rich,
and they were as ample as they were voluntary.
Thofe who were lefs opulent gave as they thought
proper, and could afford, and the poor gave nothing; for fmall tithes were then unknown. The
fame is the cafe with us Diffenters. All our places
of public worfhip are open to the poor, as well as
to the rich; and not only are the poor accommo-
dated *gratis*, but their wants are attended to as far
as the funds of the congregation (and in all of them
there is one for this purpofe) can go towards their
relief.

The inftruction of the poor is more attended to
by the Methodifts than by any other clafs of chriftians in this country. They not only make them
welcome, but they feek out, they invite, and prefs
them to receive inftruction; and if thofe of them,
who are comparatively poor, tax themfelves for the
maintenance of their preachers, and the building
of their places of worfhip, it is in fuch a manner as
promotes induftry, and checks profligacy and extra-
gance. By this means, becoming more fober, and
more frugal, they grow comparatively rich, and
are better able to contribute their penny, their
two-pence, or their fix-pence a week, to fupply the
wants of others. I honour their wifdom and œco-
nomy, and think moft highly of thofe perfons

whofe

whofe education and habits difpofe and enable them
to adapt themfelves to the inftruction of the loweft
and pooreft of the vulgar.   They are civilizing and
chriftianizing that part of the community, which
is below the notice of your dignified clergy, but
whofe fouls, as the common phrafe is, are as *pre-
cious in the fight of God*, as thofe who are called *their
betters.* Such men will have their reward in heaven.   I only wifh they had more knowledge, and
more charity along with their zeal ; and *thefe* alfo
will come in due time.

You think it equally neceffary, that public provifion fhould be made for the inftruction of the
rich, and that, in order to engage their attention and
refpect, the civil eftablifhment of religion fhould
be fplendid.   " Such fublime principles," you fay,
p. 137, "ought to be infufed into perfons in ex-
" alted fituations, and religious eftablifhments pro-
" vided that may continually revive and enforce
" them. The people of England," you fay, p. 152,
" know how little influence the teachers of religion
" are likely to have with the wealthy and power-
" ful of long ftanding, and how much lefs weight
" with the newly fortunate, if they appear no way
" afforted to thofe with whom they muft affociate,
" and over whom they muft even exercife in fome
" cafes fomething like an authority.   What muft
" they think of that body of teachers, if they fee
" it

" it in no part above the establishment of their do-
" mestic servants?"

On the effect of splendid establishments on the
minds of men I have enlarged before, and shall now
only observe that, through grofs inattention to the
principles of human nature, you have neither considered the effect of the situation in which you have
placed the clergy of this country on their own
minds, or on those of the rich and the great, to
whom their ministry is adapted. Is it not a fact,
that, so far from the former being independent of the
latter, in consequence of having great emolument
in continual prospect (which is the cafe of all the
clergy, the bishops themselves not excepted) that
they must continually look up to them, and court
them, in order to advance themselves? Is not their
attention to the great in general extremely servile
and debasing? Have you never heard of their con-
niving at, rather than reproving them for, their
vices and extravagancies, while they have the care
of their education at home, and abroad. Is not almost every clergyman, whose talents or connections
encourage him to aspire to a bishopric, or any other
great preferment, ready to adopt the maxims, and
court the favour of the great, in whose power alone
it is to aid their views ? Is it not notorious that the
bishops in general fall in with the measures of the
court, whatever they are, evidently because they
cannot

cannot rife higher, or provide for their dependants, by any other means? For whenever the maxims and meafures of the court change, the conduct of the bifhops almoft univerfally, and even inftantly, changes with them.

When, after the Court was difpofed to favour us, the diffenting minifters waited by appointment upon an archbifhop, in order to get his vote and intereft for relief in the matter of fubfcription, which was then under confideration in parliament, after both himfelf and his brethren had voted againft us upon a former occafion, he affured them that, though their bench had concurred in rejecting their application before, it was no meafure of *theirs*, but that they had been *put upon it* by the king's minifters. This he evidently thought a fufficient apology for his own conduct, and that of his brethren. So valid did this excufe appear to him, that he had no feeling of the difhonour which fuch conduct reflected upon the whole bench, and what a defpicable idea he was giving of himfelf, and of his brethren to us Diffenters, who are ufed to think and act for ourfelves, and not as we are *put upon* by others. Can fuch conduct as this, which the fituation of your dignified clergy neceffarily leads them into, infpire perfons of high rank, or of any rank, with fentiments of *refpect?* I will venture to fay it is impoffible. Pretend what you will, you muft,

and

and you do, hold them in contempt, as much as we do ourſelves. It is the feeling of indignant honour. It is the natural ſentiment of man towards his degraded fellow creature, which in ſome meaſure reflects diſhonour upon himſelf, as being of the ſame ſpecies.

You, who are a *lay divine,* farther teach us, that civil eſtabliſhments of religion are peculiarly uſeful in free governments. "The conſecration of the "ſtate," you ſay, p. 137, "by a ſtate religi- "ous eſtabliſhment, is neceſſary alſo to operate "with an wholeſome awe upon free citizens, be- "cauſe, in order to ſecure their freedom, they muſt "enjoy ſome determinate portion of power. To "them, therefore, a religion connected with the "ſtate, and with their duty towards it, becomes "even more neceſſary, than in ſuch ſocieties where "the people, by the terms of their ſubjection, are "confined to private ſentiments, and the manage- "ment of their own family concerns. All perſons "poſſeſſing any portion of power, ought to be "ſtrongly and awfully impreſſed with an idea that "they act in truſt, and that they are to account for "their conduct in that truſt to the one great maſ- "ter, author, and founder, of ſociety. This prin- "ciple ought even to be more ſtrongly impreſſed "upon the minds of thoſe who compoſe the col- "lective ſovereignty, than upon thoſe of ſingle "princes.

" princes. Without inftruments, thefe princes can
" do nothing. Whoever ufes inftruments, in find-
" ing helps, finds alfo impediments. Their power,
" therefore, is by no means complete, nor are they
" fafe in extreme abufe.———But where popular
" authority is abfolute and unftrained, the people
" have an infinitely greater, becaufe a far better
" founded, confidence in their own power.—It is
" therefore of infinite importance that they fhould
" not be fuffered to imagine that their will, any
" more than that of kings, is the ftandard of right
" and wrong, &c. &c."

In all this, Sir, you, as ufual, confound *religion*
with the *civil eftablifhment* of it, and hence the ma-
nifeft inconclufivenefs of your whole argument.
Religion, no doubt, is ufeful to all men, of all
ranks, in power, or fubject to it, as it furnifhes an
additional motive to good behaviour in every fituation. But what has this to do with any civil eftablifhment of it, with its being maintained by the
ftate, the officers of which ftate, will, of courfe,
have the fole power of ecclefiaftical as well as civil
preferment? How will the members of a popular
affembly be overawed by the admonitions of men
whofe falaries are fettled, and whofe places are difpofed of, by themfelves, any more than a fingle arbitrary fovereign? Will not the clergy always look
up to that power, which has preferment at its dif-
pofal,

poſal, in whatever hands it be lodged? Are not the eſtabliſhed miniſters in Holland advocates for their republican government, as much as the Engliſh biſhops of this day for the limited monarchy of England, and as the biſhops of Charles I. and II. were for abſolute monarchy, paſſive obedience, and non-reſiſtance?

The clergy, or any other ſet of men, in the pay of a ſtate, ſoon perceive what are the maxims of the governing powers in that ſtate, and readily adopt them. Are not the aſpiring clergy of the preſent reign, advocates for higher maxims of government in church and ſtate, than thoſe of the two preceding reigns? The fact is evident, and the difference is to be looked for in the different diſpoſitions of the courts. The former were liberal, and favourable to diſſenters, and the preſent is leſs ſo. This alone accounts for the whole. If the governors of any country in which religion is eſtabliſhed, have no motives to ſtand in awe of the miniſters of religion, which they evidently have not (as they always ſee the miniſters of religion ſtanding in awe of *them*, and courting them) it is of no uſe to them that it is eſtabliſhed at all. If it be of any uſe, it is ſimply as *religion*, as a principle operating upon conſcience, and influencing individuals, independently of any civil eſtabliſhment of it.

Indeed,

Indeed, Sir, you fee this whole bufinefs in a very wrong point of light. The civil eftablifhment of religion is fo far from making it refpectable, that it is the very thing that makes it contemptible; becaufe it naturally tends to debafe the minds of thofe who officiate in it, thofe to whom men will commonly look for examples of its proper fpirit and tendency, and by whofe principles and conduct they are too apt to form their opinion of it.

I am, DEAR SIR,

Yours, &c.

LETTER

LETTER IX.

Of an Elective Clergy.

DEAR SIR,

THE dread you exprefs of the clergy of this country becoming *elective*, is extreme, and the confequences which you imagine to flow from a regulation of this kind in the conftitution of the church, you exhibit in the moft alarming light. I fhall felect the following, as fome of the ftrongeft paffages in your publication upon this fubject, and I fhall then make a few remarks upon them.

" The prefent ruling power" (viz. of France) " has," you fay, p. 217, " made a degrading, pen-" fionary eftablifhment, to which no man of liberal " ideas, or liberal condition, will deftine his children. " It muft fettle into the loweft claffes of the peo-" ple. As with you, the inferior clergy are not " numerous enough for their duty, as thefe duties " are beyond meafure, minute, and toilfome ; as " you have left no middle claffes of clergy at their " eafe, in future nothing of fcience, or erudition, " can exift in the Gallican church. To complete " the project, without the leaft attention to the
" rights

" rights of patrons, the Affembly has provided in
" future an elective clergy; an arrangement which
" will drive out of the clerical profeffion all men of
" fobriety, all who can pretend to independence in
" their function or their conduct, and which will
" throw the whole direction of the public mind
" into the hands of a fet of licentious, bold, crafty,
" factious, flattering wretches, of fuch condition,
" and fuch habits of life, as will make their con-
" temptible penfions (in comparifon of which
" the ftipend of an excifeman is lucrative and
" honourable) an object of low and illiberal in-
" trigue."

   " In fhort," you fay, p. 218, " it feems to me, that
" this new ecclefiaftical eftablifhment, is intended only
" to be temporary, and preparatory to the utter abo-
" lition, under any of its forms, of the chriftian
" religion, whenever the minds of men are prepar-
" ed for this laft ftroke againft it, by the accom-
" plifhment of the plan for bringing its minifters
" into univerfal contempt.   I hope," you add,
p. 219, "their partizans in England, will fuc-
" ceed neither in the pillage of the ecclefiaftics,
" nor in the introduction of a principle of popu-
" lar election to our bifhoprics and parochial cures.
" This, in the prefent condition of the world,
" would be the laft corruption of the church, the
" utter ruin of the clerical character, the moft dan-
                            " gerous

" gerous ſhock that the ſtate ever received
" through a miſunderſtood arrangement of reli-
" gion."

Now, Sir, had you reflected ever ſo little on the
nature of the caſe, had you read eccleſiaſtical hiſtory, or had you opened your eyes to exiſting facts,
ſuch as almoſt obtrude themſelves upon the moſt
careleſs obſerver every day, you muſt have perceived that an *elective clergy* muſt have, always has
had, and at this preſent time actually has, effects the
very reverſe of thoſe with which your imagination
(for here *judgment* is totally out of the queſtion) is
haunted.

Is it not true that, in all caſes of a *civil* nature,
every perſon, who receives a ſalary for any duty
whatever, will be more attentive to that duty, when
the perſon who pays the ſalary, and who is intereſted
in the proper diſcharge of the duty, has the power
of appointing and diſmiſſing him? The reaſon is
obvious. It then becomes the intereſt both of the
perſon who performs the duty, and of the perſon
who is benefited by it, that it be *well done.* And can it
make any difference, whether the duty be of an
eccleſiaſtical, or a civil nature, when both are diſ-
charged by *men,* beings of the ſame paſſions, and
ſubject to the ſame influences? Every man will do
his duty beſt when he has the eye of a maſter immediately upon him. Pleaſe, Sir, to make the trial.

H H   Let

Let your domeſtic ſervants, or your domeſtic chaplain, be appointed not by yourſelf, but ſome other man, or body of men, and let it be as difficult and as ſlow a proceſs, to obtain a change of them, as it now is for a pariſh to get rid of a miniſter whoſe conduct diſgraces them, which is but too often the caſe. I do not believe that, upon this plan, you would have much expectation of being well ſerved.

You dread a ſcene of *faction*, and low *intrigue* among the clergy who ſhould be candidates for places in the church. But what was the fact for more than a thouſand years in the chriſtian church in general, when all the biſhops and clergy were elective, when *men* were the ſame as they are now, and, when whatever you imagine of peculiar zeal, and diſintereſtedneſs, in the primitive times of the church, was certainly abated? Or what is now the caſe with the Diſſenters in this country, and through all the ſtates of North America, where the officiating clergy of all denominations are now, and ever have been, elective. In ancient times, where the emoluments were great, as in the churches of Alexandria, Antioch, Conſtantinople, and Rome, the election of biſhops was ſometimes attended with factions, and dangerous ones; but even there caſes of this kind were rare, and in the ordinary ſees they ſeldom or never happened. There are more than a thouſand diſſenting miniſters in this kingdom, and

they

they are all elected by their respective congregations; but any great inconvenience attending an election of this kind very seldom occurs. It is probable that you, though living in the country, never heard of any such thing, any more than in America, or among the dissenters in Ireland.

So far is there from being any cabal, or intrigue, to obtain places with us, that the person chosen seldom hears of it, till his invitation is sent to him; and any thing like *canvassing* would be an effectual bar to his election. Indeed, it very seldom happens that there is more than one candidate named at one time, and the members of any congregation are considered as very imprudent if they admit of two.

You say, that no person liberally educated, or any other than those in the lowest classes of life, will be candidates for church preferment. This, Sir, goes upon the idea that no person will officiate in a christian church but for the sake of the temporal emolument which he receives from it, which is a most unjust and ill-founded reflection on christianity, and the ministers of it. It may be the case with a church, the articles of which men of sense cannot subscribe, and the stated duty of which is against their consciences. For such services as *these* men must be *paid*, and very well paid too; and in general it will be done for nothing but the pay. But

this

this is not the cafe with *us*, nor was it fo in the early ages of the church. Though few of our falaries will more than half maintain us, there are never wanting perfons of independent fortune, and the moft liberal education, who voluntarily devote themfelves to the work of our miniftry. From unbiaffed choice they give their time, and their fortunes, to an employment which they deem to be moft honourable and important, in whatever light it may appear to *you*; and our fituation is fuch, that few befides perfons of fome ability and piety will think of the profeffion.

So refpected is the character of a minifter with us, though the cafe may be different with you, that whatever was his original rank in life, it places him on a level with the moft opulent of his congregation; and it rarely happens but that, in all our congregations, there are fome perfons of as good fortunes, and as polifhed manners, as any others in the town or neighbourhood. On this account, as well as from a principle of genuine piety and benevolence, the fituation of a diffenting minifter has many attractions, efpecially to a perfon of a ferious and ftudious turn of mind. We think it greatly preferable to that of the generality of the eftablifhed clergy, with all their profpects of preferment, which often produce a cringing and fervile difpofition. And I will venture to fay, that, independent of the private fortunes

which

which many of our minifters have, their character
and conduct render them as truly refpectable, and
independent in mind, as any fet of clergy in the
world; far more fo, I am confident, than yours, with
all the advantages you boaft.

In confequence of the bifhops in France becoming elective, you imagine that nothing of *ſcience*,
or *erudition*, will henceforth exift in the Gallican
church. But did nothing of this kind exift in the
chriftian church before the bifhops ceafed to be
elective, which was a change made of late years in
comparifon? Hiftory fhews the very reverfe to have
been the cafe. The dignified clergy, whom the court
makes independent of the people, are not thofe who,
in any country, produce learned theological works,
but generally men in the lower orders, and who have
no motive to chufe their profeffion befides an attachment to the duties and ftudies peculiar to it, and
who wifh to diftinguifh themfelves in it. Very few
of the bifhops of your church have been writers,
at leaft after they were made bifhops. The greateft
works your church has to boaft of were the pro-
ductions of obfcure clergymen; and, defpicable as
our fituation may appear to you, who certainly
know very little about us, an application to the
ftudies fuited to our profeffion, appears, by the
number of our writings, to be much greater than
among the clergy of the eftablifhed church. The

H 3

relation we ftand in to our congregations infures a refpectable private character, and in a manner obliges us to devote the leifure we have to literature, to fcience, and to profeffional ftudies. How ftrangely, Sir, muft you be blinded by your high church prejudices not to perceive that this both is, and neceffarily *muft be* the difference between the clergy of the eftablifhed church, and minifters with us; a difference greatly to our advantage; and it arifes wholly from our people having the choice of their minifters, and of courfe a power of difmiffing them when, on any account, they do not approve of them.

You infinuate that the fcheme to render the clergy of France elective, is preparatory to an intended abolition of chriftianity, as if chriftianity did not exift, and exift in infinitely greater purity, before any of the clergy were otherwife than elective. On the contrary, it is the fyftem of church eftablifhments that always has produced, and that ever muft produce, unbelievers. You make it a mere engine of ftate, a fource of *wealth* to fome of the clergy, and of *power* to thofe who have the nomination of them; and in both cafes the proper interefts of *religion* are never thought of. In confequence of this, it is notorious that the fuperior clergy in France and Italy, have long been generally confidered as unbelievers, as well as thofe who procure them

them their preferment. That the church of England is not exempt from the fame cenfure, I have actually known myfelf; and it is highly probable that, from fimilar caufes, it ftill exifts in a degree which I have now no opportunity of knowing. Yet though you clearly fee that a fplendid church eftablifhment, with bifhops appointed by the court, actually makes many of the clergy mere *men of the world*, fo that they have nothing of the *chriftian minifter*, befides the name, and the confequence of this has been the difbelief and utter contempt of chriftianity in men of rank and fortune, you would pretend that the abolifhing of chriftianity would be the confequence of their diffolution. Indeed, Sir, both the nature of the cafe, and facts, which are obvious to the moft carelefs eye, fhew that chriftianity cannot be preferved along with them. They are a difeafe that muft be extirpated, or the fubject will be deftroyed.

I am, DEAR SIR,

Yours, &c.

LETTER

LETTER X.

Of Monaſtic Inſtitutions, and Mr. Burke's general Maxim that exiſting Powers are not to be deſtroyed.

DEAR SIR,

YOU enlarge much, p. 234, &c. on the ill policy of the National Aſſembly of France,
in diſſolving the *monaſtic inſtitutions* of that country,
acknowledging, at the ſame time, that " they favour
" of ſuperſtition. This," you ſay, " ought not,
" however, to hinder them from deriving from ſu-
" perſtition itſelf any reſources which from thence
" may be furniſhed for the public advantage." You
do not ſay what uſes, religious or political, you
would have made of the funds of theſe ſocieties;
but as you acknowledge that " the body of all true
" religion conſiſts in obedience to the will of the
" Sovereign of the univerſe, in a confidence in his
" declarations, and in an imitation of his perfec-
" tions," it is ſufficient, I ſhould think, for a ſtate to
provide for *this*. If the ſtate give the *body*, let the
individuals themſelves provide the *cleathing*, and to
what

what better ufe can public lands and funds be applied, than to liquidate the debts of a ftate ?

Monaftic inftitutions have, no doubt, had their ufes, and very great ufes, when there was no other retreat for letters, or from the buftle of a barbarous age. But as literature and piety do not now want that afylum, and every purpofe of ufeful religion may be gained as well, and even better, without it, what reafon can there be for its continuance ? Why preferve an old and inconvenient road, when a better is actually gained ? Rather convert it into good arable or pafture land.

It is, befides, impoffible to encourage fuperftition, but at the expence of true religion, as the experience of every age demonftrates. The duties of fuperftition are better defined than thofe of religion. Men know precifely when they have recited a certain number of prayers, or when they have received a certain number of lafhes ; but the great duties of benevolence (which, indeed, can only be difcharged in fociety) are indefinite, and withal require an attention to the *inward temper of mind,* which is far more difficult than any of the injunctions of fuperftition. Will it not be natural, then, for men to attach themfelves to the one, and neglect the other, efpecially when they are

taught

taught that the same end may be gained by ei-ther?

The very *principle* upon which monachism is founded, is false and delusive. It is that men, capable of performing the duties of life, may become fit for heaven by solitary meditation and prayer, without mixing with the world at all. While monasteries are kept up, this idea is encouraged. I cannot help thinking, therefore, that the National Assembly acted very wisely, when, in order to relieve themselves from the difficulties which the folly and extravagance of a former government had brought upon the country, they adopted the measure of abolishing their monasteries, making however a sufficient provision for the inhabitants of them.

You will not pretend to say that monastic institutions are any necessary part of the christian system, since no mention is made of any such thing in the New Testament, since such establishments as you lament the fall of, are, in fact, but recent things, and since christianity has not been found to suffer any thing by the demolition of them in this, or any other protestant country.

But " in monastic institutions," you say, p. 232, " in my opinion, was found a great power for the " mechanism of politic benevolence. There were " reve-

" revenues with a public direction; there were
" men wholly set apart and educated to public pur-
" poses, without any other than public ties, and
" public principles; men without a possibility of
" converting the estate of the community into a
" private fortune; men denied to self interest, whose
" avarice is for the community; men to whom
" personal poverty is honour, and implicit obe-
" dience stands in the place of freedom. In vain
" shall a man look to the possibility of making such
" things when he wants them. The winds blow
" as they list. These institutions are the products
" of enthusiasm; they are the instruments of wif-
" dom. Wisdom cannot create materials, they are
" the gifts of nature, or chance; her pride is in the
" use. To destroy any power," you say, p. 233,
" growing wild from the rank productive force of
" the human mind, is almost tantamount in the
" moral world, to the destruction of the apparently
" active properties of bodies in the material. Had
" you no way of using the men, but by convert-
" ing monks into pensioners?"

Upon this principle, of no *power* being to be
destroyed, but only to be *regulated*, the greatest abuses
may be perpetuated; because, in many cases, there
is no preventing the abuse, without destroying the
power itself. Such, for example, is the claim of

the

the Popes to univerſal dominion over the chriſtian church, and even over temporal princes; in fact, the aſſumption of *all power in heaven and in earth.* Such, alſo, is the power of a prieſt to give abſolution of ſins. To you it ſignifies nothing to allege, that theſe were altogether, and from the beginning, *innovations* and *abuſes* in the chriſtian ſyſtem. You anſwer that they were *great powers, which cannot be created at pleaſure,* and therefore that a wiſe ſtatesman would be an advocate for their preſervation, and not for their deſtruction.

To adopt your mode of reaſoning, ſuch deep rooted opinions, as formerly prevailed in all the chriſtian world, of an immenſe power lodged for the wiſeſt purpoſes in one viſible head of the church, the ſublime idea of one *ſpiritual father of all chriſtian princes,* who had no other bond of union, and who ſtood in great need of one, and the confidence that all chriſtians once had in the abſolving power of their prieſts, authoriſed to give advice and direction in all caſes in which *conſcience* was concerned ; ſuch opinions as theſe, you will ſay, cannot be produced at pleaſure, they were the ſlow growth of ages, and a foundation of *great powers,* which, if once deſtroyed, will never riſe again. It was, therefore, nothing elſe than madneſs, you would ſay, in the firſt reformers, to aim at the ſubverſion

of

of thefe powers, by refuting the opinions on which they were founded. They fhould have contented themfelves with preferving thefe powers, facred and inviolable, and have contrived how to make a right ufe of them.

For the fame reafon, had you, in any country, as in Morocco, found the idea of the abfolute power in the prince, the facrednefs of his perfon, and the happinefs of dying by his hand, you would have been careful not to deftroy that *power*, which you might not be able to re-produce; but, being happily in poffeffion of it, would have made it fubfervient to the good of the country.

I am glad, however, to find that, though all powers are to be *continued*, you allow of fome improvement in the *application* of them, which implies fome change for the better. This is alfo implied in what you fay by way of apology for the old church eftablifhment of France, p. 206, that " it " was an old one, and not frequently revifed," as if fome *revifal*, at leaft, would have been proper. And if a revifal of *this* eftablifhment would have been proper, why not that of *ours* alfo? Has the church of England acquired any prefcriptive right, to ftand in no need of any farther revifion; or are you, Sir, authorifed to fay to reformation, *Hitherto fhalt thou go, and no farther?* If not, why your
fneers,

sneers, p. 14, at a certain *lay divine*, who only pro-
posed a revisal of the English liturgy and articles,
which, in the opinion of many serious and thinking
persons, though not in yours, very much want revision? Why, also, did you oppose the petition of
a number of conscientious clergymen, to be releas-
ed from their present obligation to subscribe to the
thirty-nine articles, many of which you must yourself, surely, think are not absolutely essential to christianity? Why, then, might not clergymen, as well
as others, have been at liberty to speculate freely,
and think as they saw reason to do, with respect
to them?

On the same principles on which you opposed a
revision of the church establishment of *this* country, you would, no doubt, have opposed a revision of that of France, of Turkey, or of Indostan.
However, the spirit of reformation, which is now
gone forth, is *another great power*, as well as the
existing systems to be reformed by it; and it is a
power which grows stronger as they grow weaker;
so that there can be no doubt which of them will
finally prevail, notwithstanding the aid that your
potent arm may give them.

You boldly avow your attachment to old establishments, because they are old. " In this en-
" lightened age," you say, p. 129, " I am bold
                                    " enough

" enough to confess, that we are generally men of
" untaught feelings, that, instead of casting away
" all our old prejudices, we cherish them to a very
" considerable degree, and to take more shame to
" ourselves, we cherish them because they are pre-
" judices; and the longer they have lasted, and
" the more generally they have prevailed, the more
" we cherish them."

On this principle, Sir, had you been a Pagan at
the time of the promulgation of christianity, you
would have continued one. You would also have
opposed the reformation. You would, no doubt,
have cherished the long and deep rooted prejudice
of the earth being the center of our system, and
every notion that was *old*; the creed of your nurse,
and of your grandmother, in opposition to every
thing *new*.

Cherish them, then, Sir, as much as you please.
Prejudice and error is only a *mist*, which the sun,
which has now risen, will effectually disperse.
Keep them about you as tight as the countryman
in the fable did his cloak; the same sun, without
any more violence than the warmth of his beams,
will compel you to throw it aside, unless you chuse
to sweat under it, and bear the ridicule of all your
cooler and less encumbered companions. The
spirit of free and rational enquiry is now abroad,

and

and without any aid from the powers of this world, will not fail to overturn all error and falſe religion, wherever it is found, and neither the church of Rome, nor the church of England, will be able to ſtand before it.

Inſtead of your chimerical idea of *deſtroying no exiſting powers*, but of converting them to ſome *uſe*, which may anſwer no better than an attempt to tame a lion, or a tiger, adopt a plainer maxim, infinitely better adapted to the weak faculties of man, viz. to *follow truth wherever it leads you*, confident that the intereſts of truth will ever be inſeparable from thoſe of virtue and happineſs, and equally ſo to ſtates, as to individuals.

I am, DEAR SIR,

Yours, &c.

LETTER

L E T T E R XI.

Of the Sacredness of the Revenues of the Church.

DEAR SIR,

YOUR opinion of the *sacredness*, and *majesty*, of an established church, is most conspicuous in what you say of its *revenues*. On this subject you appear to have adopted maxims, which, I believe, were never before avowed by any Protestant, viz. that the state has no power or authority over any thing, that has once been the property of the church.

" From the united consideration of religion and " constitutional policy," you say, p. 150, " from " their opinion of a duty to make a sure provision " for the consolation of the feeble, and the instruc- " tion of the ignorant, they have incorporated and " identified the estate of the church with the " mass of private property, of which the state " is not the *proprietor*, either for *use* or *domi-* " *nion*, but the *guardian* only, and the *regu-* " *later*. They have ordained that the provision of " this establishment might be as stable as the earth

I " on

" on which it ſtands, and ſhould not fluctuate with
" the Euripus of funds and actions."

If the ſtate be not the *proprietor* of the church
lands, they muſt be the abſolute *unalienable property*
of the *church*, that is of *churchmen* only, and without
their conſent no alienation of them is lawful.   Con-
ſequently, if all the members of the Houſe of Commons, the king, and all the temporal lords, ſhould
vote the alienation of any part of them, it would be
mere *robbery* without the conſent of the biſhops,
or perhaps that of the whole convocation aſſembled
for the purpoſe ; perhaps not even then, the preſent clergy being only *truſtees*, or having a *life
eſtate* in a revenue which belongs to their ſucceſſors.
But, ſurely, if I have any knowledge of the Britiſh
conſtitution, this doctrine is abſolutely new to it,
and certainly not deduced from the actual conduct
of parliament, which has diſpoſed of a very great
proportion of what was once the property of the
church.   I even queſtion whether the principle you
here avow, would at this day be acknowledged at
St. Omers.   The Catholics of France had evidently no idea of the kind, and indeed it is for this that
you reproach them.

The Dutch, and other proteſtant ſtates, have confiſcated all the old church property, and pay their
clergy from the ſame public treaſury, out of which
the officers of the army and navy are paid ; and
they,

they, no doubt, think themfelves juftified in fo doing.   A great proportion of the tithes in this country, and, as I am informed, the whole of them in
Scotland, is now in the hands of lay proprietors,
who, in your opinion, muft all be guilty of *facri-
lege*, though their conduct be fanctioned by the law
of the land.

If the right of the church to its revenues is not
to be affected by any act of a civil legiflature, if
this right be not derived from any *ordinance of man*,
it muft come to them from the *ordinance of God*.
But where, Sir, do you find any record of this?
There is no mention made of tithes, or of any per-
manent church property, in the New Teftament;
and if it has been by the ordinance of God in any
period fubfequent to the writing of thofe books, it
is incumbent upon you, Sir, and other advocates
for the unalienable property of the church, to fhew
when the grant was made, and by what miracle
(for nothing elfe can anfwer the purpofe) it was
confirmed.   But every thing relative to the revenues of the church, is eafily traced in hiftory.   We
very well know *when*, and *whence*, every branch of
it arofe.   It was altogether the ordinance of *men*,
and generally of weak, fuperftitious, and prieft-
ridden men.   And furely the mifchiefs which have
been found to arife from the folly of one age, ought

to be removed by the wifdom of a fubfequent one. In one paffage, indeed, you allow all that I contend for, when you fay, p. 154, " When once the com-" mon-wealth has eftablifhed the eftates of the " church as property;" for this implies that the eftates of the church are the gift of the common-wealth, or ftate ; and what the ftate has *given*, it may furely *take away*.   This is one, among many inconfiftencies, in your work.

Such, I flatter myfelf, is the light of the prefent day, that, confident as you are of your maxim, and of the members of our legiflature acting upon it, you will fome time or other find yourfelf mif-taken. " The Commons of Great Britain," you fay, p. 156, " in a national emergency, will never " feek their refource from the confifcation of the " eftates of the church and poor. Sacrilege and " profcription are not among the ways and means " of our committee of fupply. The Jews, in " Change-alley, have not yet dared to hint their " hopes of a mortgage on the revenues belonging " to the fee of Canterbury. I am not afraid that I " fhall be difavowed, when I affure you, that there " is not *one* public man in this kingdom whom " you would wifh to quote, no not one of any party " or defcription, who does not reprobate the dif-" honeft, perfidious, and cruel confifcation which

" the

" the National Affembly has been compelled to
" make, of that property which it was their firft
" duty to protect."

I am furprized, Sir, that you fhould not be fenfible that this declaration is by no means true in
fact. It is in my own power to quote many perfons in public life, who greatly approve that conduct of the National Affembly of France which
you fo ftrongly condemn. You forget that *Salus
Reipublicæ eft fuprema lex*; and if ever the circumftances of this country fhould be fuch, as that either
the intereft of the *church* or the *ftate* muft be aban-
doned, I have no doubt but the former would be
readily facrificed to the latter.

You have made the provifion for the *poor* as facred as that for the *church*. But certainly this was
the inftitution of *man*, or rather of *woman*; for it
took its rife in the time of queen Elizabeth, in this
country, and is not known in any other. To many
perfons, as well as to myfelf, our method of providing
for the poor, is no proof of the wifdom of our
anceftors. It takes from man the neceffity of *fore-
fight*, and inftead of being the moft provident,
makes him the moft improvident of all creatures.
So far are our poor laws from encouraging induftry,
that they encourage idlenefs, and of courfe profligacy. Such is the ftate of this country, burthened
with taxes to fupport the church, and the poor, and

I 3

to pay the intereſt (the principal is out of the queſtion) of debts contracted by the folly of our anceſtors, that its ability to ſupport itſelf under them, is very problematical *.

" It is," you ſay, p. 149, " from our attach-
" ment to a church eſtabliſhment, that the Engliſh
" nation did not think it wiſe to intruſt that great
" fundamental intereſt of the whole, to what they
" truſt no part of their civil or military public
" ſervice, that is, to the unſteady and precarious
" contribution of individuals.   They go farther.
" They certainly never have ſuffered, and never
" will ſuffer, the fixed eſtate of the church to be
" converted into a penſion, to depend on the Trea-
" ſury, &c.   The people of England think that
" they have conſtitutional motives, as well as re-
" ligious, againſt any project of turning their inde-
" pendent clergy into eccleſiaſtical penſioners of
" ſtate.   They tremble for their liberty, from the
" influence of a clergy dependent on the crown;
" they tremble for the public tranquility, from the
" diſorders of a factious clergy, if it were made to
" depend upon any other than the crown.   They

---

* Would it not be reaſonable to fix ſome time, beyond which it ſhould not be deemed right to bind poſterity ? If our anceſtors make a fooliſh *law*, we ſcruple not to repeal it ; but if they make fooliſh *wars*, and incur fooliſh *debts*, we have, at preſent, no re-medy whatever.

" therefore

" therefore made their church, like their king, and
" their nobility, independent."

There are several positions in this paragraph,
that appear to me rather extraordinary. The
clergy, to be as independent as the crown, or the
nobility, should have a negative in all proceedings
in parliament. But the clergy are, in fact, dependent upon the crown, and must necessarily be
so, while the crown has the disposal of all bishop-
rics, and other great preferments ; and the effect
of this is seen by their voting with the crown. It
is also no compliment to the general disposition of
the clergy, that you should tremble for the effects
of their *factions*, if they were to depend upon any
other than the crown. I should think, however,
that, if they be so dangerous a body of men, you
might make yourself rather easier if they were made
to depend on the *whole legislature*, and not upon
the crown only, to which they now give a dangerous accession of power.

But, Sir, only take away the emoluments of
the clergy, and leave them to subsist, as we dissenting ministers do, and as the apostles and bishops
in primitive times did, on the voluntary contributions of those who are benefited by their ministry,
and you will effectually remove all cause of trem-
bling on their account. Let them be naturally as

I 4   quarrelsome

quarrelfome as dogs, they will be as quiet as lambs, if no bone of contention be thrown among them. What danger arifes from *our* divifions, or thofe of the many difcordant fects which have ever exifted in North America? Be they ever fo great, we never trouble the ftate with them, and we are unanimous and hearty in every common caufe, refpecting either chriftianity or public liberty.

I am, Dear Sir,

Yours, &c.

LETTER XII.

Of the Danger of the Church, and of the Test Laws.

DEAR SIR,

THE cry of the *church being in danger*, is almost as old as the church itself, and has been kept up by its friends, and physicians, whenever it has suited their purpose, from the earliest times to the present day. This has served as an excuse for every outrage upon others; as if nothing was ever meant by them, but to secure itself. And thus the most bloody and *offensive* wars are often made under the cover of being merely *defensive* ones, which are always held to be lawful. Now, had this church of yours, whose fears and cries have always been the signal of alarm to all its neighbours, being made of proper materials, and constructed in a proper manner, it would never have had any thing to fear. The *church of Christ* is built upon a rock, and we are assured that *the gates of hell shall not prevail against it.* Had your church been built upon this rock of truth, it would have had nothing to fear. Its own evidence and excellence would have supported it.

I

Should

Should the *ſtate* itſelf be overturned, the people would, of themſelves, and from predilection, rein-ſtate their favourite *church* in all its former rights and privileges. But you are ſenſible it has not this hold on the minds of the people, and you juſtly ſuſpect that, if any misfortune ſhould happen to it, they would never rebuild it, but, if left to their own free choice, would adopt ſome other plan, more uſeful and commodious.

Time was when your church pretended to *fear where no fear was,* and being then vigorous, her cries were heard as the roaring of a lion. Of late ſhe has been ſo feeble, that we only amuſe ourſelves with them; and now the danger is really tranſ-ferred from us to herſelf.

As you, Sir, are ſo *tremblingly alive all over,* for the fate of this dear church of yours, I will tell you two real cauſes of apprehenſion with reſpect to it, the one from without, and the other from within.

I. Be afraid of war, or any thing that ſhall add to the public burdens. For whenever the time ſhall come that the intereſt of the national debt can-not be paid (and that time certainly approaches) ſacred as the property of the church might be in your pious hands, in whoſe mind, as you ſay, p. 147, " a continued and general approbation of " the church eſtabliſhment is ſo worked, that you
" are

" are not able to diftinguifh what you have learned
" from others from the refult of your own medita-
" tions;" other perfons, having had a different education, may be able to make this diftinction, and
without any dread of divine judgments, may, while
you ftand aghaft with horror, and expiring with dif-
may, apply the hallowed treafure to fome unhallowed
ufe. Had our prefent minifter actually entered
into the war that fome fuppofe he did not do wifely
to provoke, and the confequence had been, as it
probably would, the addition of another hundred
millions to our debt, though *you* might not tremble
for what you confider as the *ark of God* in this country, other perfons, whofe faith was not fo ftrong,
certainly would.

You, Sir, appear not to be infenfible of the new
and critical fituation into which immenfe public
debts have brought moft European nations, our
own not excepted. The apparent ftability of thefe
governments has encouraged them to venture upon
a fyftem, which, by calling forth the powers of future generations in aid of the prefent, has enabled
them to make extraordinary exertions on particular
occafions. Had there been wifdom in thefe exertions, pofterity, being benefited by them, would
have reafon to thank their anceftors. But exertions of this kind exceeding the natural powers of the ftate, have refembled thofe convulfive
motions of the mufcles which exhauft their force,

and

and debilitate them with refpect to future exertions. And if this fyftem be purfued, as in all probability it will, the time muft come when even thefe extraordinary refources will fail, and we fhall then find ourfelves in the very fame difficulties in which the French are involved at prefent.

In this cafe (which it behoves us to be looking forward to, that we may collect all our wifdom in order to leffen the danger with which it threatens us) do you imagine, Sir, that we fhall be able to preferve our prefent government in all its forms, civil and ecclefiaftical, any more than the French have been able to preferve theirs? Do not flatter yourfelf fo much. That great crifis will be the touchftone to our government, as well as to that of France. Whatever fhall be then thought to be *unfound* in the conftitution, and to have contributed, directly or indirectly, to bring us into our difficulties, will be marked for excifion, and if we muft, as it were, *begin again,* as the French have found themfelves under a neceffity of doing, we fhall, no doubt, endeavour to begin upon a better plan, and retain as few as poffible of the imperfections of which we now complain, and fhall then complain of more.

Is it not our immenfe public debt, that has in various ways contributed to the encreafed *power of the crown* (of which you, Sir, among others, not long ago complained) and is it poffible, then, that *this* fhould continue the fame, when this debt, which

now

now fupports it, can no longer be fupported? Is not our prefent fhamefully *unequal reprefentation* another circumftance connected with the power of the crown, giving it a decided majority in the Houfe of Commons? Can this, therefore, be continued, when the power of the crown is diminifhed; and will not thefe great changes in the civil conftitution be followed by many others?

In this neceffary reformation of the *civil* government, will it be poffible, think you, to prevent all enquiry into *ecclefiaftical* matters, which are now fo clofely connected with things of a civil nature? In this cafe, is it a certainty that *any* church eftablifhment will be continued; or if there be, will it be precifely that which now fubfifts? Will the bifhops retain their feats in Parliament? Will the fpiritual courts be continued? Will the clergy be maintained by tithes? Will the doctrines of the church undergo no change? Will the fubfcription to all the thirty-nine articles be ftill enforced? Will the univerfities remain fhut to the Diffenters, who cannot fubfcribe to them? Will the teft laws remain in force, to exclude us from all civil offices, &c. &c. &c.? If this be your opinion, *great*, indeed, Sir, *is your faith*, greater, I imagine, than that of many an archbifhop. Though however, it fhould be equal to the *removing* of all thefe *mountains*, you will, I doubt not, imagine this favourite church of yours to be rather fafer in times of *peace*, and without any farther encreafe of our national debt, than with a *war* that might double it.

II. This danger from *without* is uncertain, and may be warded off; but not fo that from *within*. I mean the growing light of the age, in confequence of which we are more and more fenfible of the abfurdity of the doctrines, the infufficiency of the difcipline, and the oppreffion of the revenues, of your church. The people of this country will at length difcover that what they have paid fo dearly for, as a *benefit*, is really a *nuifance*, that it is hoftile to the cleareft truth, and fubverfive of rational liberty, that very liberty for which you, Sir, profefs to be a warm advocate.

Diffenters of one denomination or other, are very much increafed of late years, and many of them are avowedly hoftile to every eftablifhment. The methodifts are by no means attached to it. Few of them ever trouble your churches, and frequently in great bodies become diffenters; and the far greater part of the nominal churchmen only hold to the church from form and cuftom; the more ferious and intelligent of them earneftly wifhing for a change, but defirous of promoting it without noife or rifk. Few perfons of rank attend your worfhip, or any worfhip, and are only attached to the church for fecular purpofes. But this and every thing elfe, fhort of a real approbation and predilection,

lection, are uncertain and poor props for so old and decayed a building as yours is.

The increase of dissenters is a fact that you and your clergy are either wholly ignorant of, or are strangely inattentive to. I shall mention only one instance. I have resided in Birmingham only ten years, and there are now building the eighth, ninth, and tenth, new places of dissenting or methodist worship, besides another building converted into a place of worship, in this town, all within this short period, nine of them for new congregations, and the others for increased ones. Another is talked of, and many have been built in the neighbourhood; and in this time there has not been one additional church, or chapel, for the members of the church of England. The increase of the dissenters and methodists in Sheffield, in Leeds, and, I have no doubt, in other manufacturing towns, has been nearly in the same proportion.

Every controversy in which churchmen have meddled has been to their disadvantage. The heads of the church therefore now wisely discourage all controversy, but even this policy will not avail them long. Every clergyman is not wise, and *fools*, as they say, *will be meddling*; and every meddling is to their hurt, and that of their cause.

Let thinking people, then, judge what must be the fate of a church, whose fundamental doctrines are difbelieved by men of fenfe and inquiry, whofe articles are well known not to be fubfcribed *bonâ fide* by thofe who officiate in it, while the truly enlightened and ferious either keep out of the church, or relinquifh their preferment in it. And this is very much the cafe with the church of England at prefent.

The alliance of any ftate with fo weak and tottering a church as yours muft either be diffolved, or both muft fall together. And, aftonifhed as you are at " the fteady eye with which" you fay, p. 85, " we are prepared to view the greateft calamity " that can befal this country," the diffolution of this fatal alliance is ftill the objeft of our moft ardent wifhes. By the calmeft reprefentations, and the moft earneft remonftrances, we are endeavouring to bring about a peaceable feparation, attended with no calamity. We have therefore nothing to blame ourfelves for, if that calamity, which we forefee, and deplore, but which the obftinacy of others may put it out of our power to prevent, fhould come. Happy is fuch a country as America, where no fuch alliance as that of church and ftate was ever formed, where no fuch unnatural mixture of ecclefiaftical and civil polity was ever made. They fee our errors, and wifely avoid them. We alfo may fee them, but when it will be too late.

You

You, Sir, who with many others have lately joined in the cry of the church being in danger, have thought to guard it by *laws and tests*, excluding Diffenters from all places of truft and profit. Paying our full fhare to the public taxes, and having always diftinguifhed ourfelves by our induftry, in manufactures and commerce (all our trading towns abounding with Diffenters) we thought it not unreafonable to requeft a right of admiffion, at the will of the crown, or the election of our fellow fubjects, to fuch advantages as arife from that flourifhing ftate of the country to which, it is not denied that, we have eminently contributed. Thrice we have made the application, and twice you, Sir, made no oppofition to us. We therefore flattered ourfelves that, having been in other refpects a friend to *equal liberty*, efpecially in America and Ireland, and Scotland alfo, where no fuch tefts are known, you would have been a friend to *us*. But it feems that, after deeply ruminating on the fubject, and having, no doubt, prayed for, and as you thought obtained, more light than you had before, you moft unexpectedly, and with peculiar warmth and fiercenefs, oppofed us *.

* Let Mr. Burke's conduct with refpect to the Teft Act, be compared with the following paffage in his prefent pamphlet. " You do not imagine that I wifh to confine power, authority, and " diftinction, to blood, and names, and titles. No Sir, there is

K "no

As you have given some attention to the case of the dissenters, and, in your speech in our favour, complained of the hardship of our being obliged to subscribe to the articles of the church, from which we derive no emolument, I wonder that you do not likewise see the unreasonableness of our being subjected to any other hardship on the same principle. As we derive no *advantage* from the established church, we ought not to suffer any unnecessary *disadvantage* from our nonconformity to it. But we certainly do so, if we be excluded from all civil offices and emoluments on that account. Must the members of this favourite church of yours, engross all the good things of *this life* as well as those of *another*, and must we unfortunate Dissenters partake of neither?

That there is danger threatening your church, I clearly see. But the method you have adopted has no tendency to lessen, but only to increase that danger. The old adage, which you had forgotten is *divide et impera*; but by holding us all out as equally

---

" no qualification for government but true virtue and wisdom.
" Wherever they are actually found, they have, in whatever state,
" condition, profession, or trade, the passport of heaven to human
" place, and honour. Woe to the country which would madly
" and impiously reject the service of the talents and virtues, civil,
" military, or religious, that are given to grace, or to serve it, and
" would condemn to obscurity every thing formed to diffuse lustre
" and glory around a state." p. 74.

objects

objects of exclusion from places of truft and power, you give us a common intereft, and a *bond of union*, which we hardly thought of before. Far from being difcouraged by our repulfes, we fhall not fail to renew our application with more confidence than ever, feeing nothing but juftice on our fide, and jealous bigotry on yours.

Had you admitted us to an equal participation of civil rights, we might have thought lefs of our religious ones. Indeed, perfons who are candidates for *civil offices* are not apt to be zealous in matters of *religion*; or if they were, the Diffenters in office being greatly out-numbered by the members of the eftablifhed church, in the fame or fimilar offices, and divided among themfelves, their power of hurting the ftate would have been nothing. A child in politics might have feen this, but you, Sir, did not.

You alfo did not fee that, what we moft of all wifh, and what you have the greateft reafon to dread, is not any temporal power, or influence, that we have any chance of acquiring. This we think little about, but *difcuffion*, the free difcuffion of every thing relating to religion. For, diftant as they may appear in idea, all religious fubjects have a relation to each other, the doctrine of the teft and that of the trinity, the power of a juftice of peace and that of a bifhop or archbifhop. Touch but any

K 2

extremity

extremity of the web, and the vibration will be felt to the center, and to every other extremity.

Your clergy themfelves force this upon us. For they cannot rail at us as Diffenters, but they muft needs glance at our *opinions*, and efpecially fuch as they imagine will render us moft obnoxious, never forgetting *unitarianifm*. Confequently, when we defend ourfelves, not being apt to entertain doubts of the goodnefs of our caufe, we purfue our antagonifts through the whole field of their argument. We boldly affert the *unity of God*, and the purity and fimplicity of his worfhip. We exclaim againft all ufurpation of the rights of our only law-giver Jefus Chrift, by priefts or kings, by councils or parliaments. On thefe topics we are always ready to *cry aloud and not fpare*. In this manner, Sir, you raife a ftorm the force of which you and your church will not be able to ftand.

It is amufing to obferve how very differently the fame things ftrike different perfons, according to their previous educations and habits of thinking. Dr. Price advifes thofe who object to the religion prefcribed by public authority, and who yet cannot altogether approve of any other, that is openly profeffed in their country, to fet up a feparate worfhip for themfelves. To me nothing appears more reafonable than this conduct; and yet you, Sir, endeavour, p. 15, to turn it into ridicule; no doubt,

ı   becaufe

becaufe to you it really appears in a ridiculous light. But *ridicule is not the teft of truth*, and if reafon and common fenfe is to be heard, it muft furely appear even to yourfelf, if you reflect a moment on the fub- ject, that upon any other principle than that of Dr. Price, no reformation can be juftified. Becaufe, upon the **very** fame principle, whatever it be, that any perfon is authorifed to diffent from a mode of worfhip fet up by the ftate, he is authorifed to diffent from any that may be fet up by private perfons; and if he think the public profeffion of religion in the form of *public worfhip* to be a duty, he is obliged in confcience to fet up one of his own, whether more or fewer perfons, or any befides his own family, will join him in it. And where, Sir, would be the great inconvenience of mafters of families, of what- ever rank, being *priefts* as well as *kings* in their own houfhold? What is there in the duty of a teacher of chriftianity, that you, Sir, are not qualified to dif- charge? And this age furnifhes abundant helps for thofe who are not qualified. If any thing elfe be an obftruction to this fcheme, it muft arife from the influence of mere fafhion, or fuperftition.

You, Sir, feem to dread a *number of fects* among chriftians. But what ferious inconvenience would arife from their being increafed even ten fold? It would be much better for the ftate, than if there were only two. Religious bigotry would alfo be

diminifhed

diminifhed by this means, and the members of thefe fects would fooner learn to exercife charity for each other, diftinguifhing the great things in which all chriftians agree, from the comparatively fmaller things in which any of them differ. In this way, alfo, they would fooner arrive at a *rational unifor-mity*; the points of difference being freely can-vaffed, and truth prevailing, and eftablifhing itfelf, as, no doubt, it will in the end.

I am now, Sir, about to relieve your attention, and that of our readers, to the fubject of the *con-nexion*, or, as it is called, the *alliance*, between the church and the ftate, but I cannot wholly conclude without expreffing my earneft wifh that it may be thoroughly confidered in every point of view.

It certainly opens a field of very important dif-cuffion for philofophers, politicians, and divines; and it is not to be treated in an authoritative dogma-tical way. That chriftian minifters fhould be paid by the ftate, rather than by thofe who chufe to be inftructed by them; that they ought to have temporal courts, with the power of inflicting civil penalties; that princes fhould have the nomination of them; that fome of them fhould be equal in rank and power to temporal peers; and that arti-cles of faith fhould have the fanction of a tem-poral legiflature, are by no means *axioms*, or felf evident truths, in a fyftem of civil policy. There muft, muſt, therefore, be more *ſimple principles*, from which, if they be proper expedients in government, their neceſſity, or expedience, may be deduced. Let us then ſee what thoſe principles are, and in what manner the deduction is made.

It cannot be ſaid, that the neceſſity, or expedience, of this mixture of civil and eccleſiaſtical power is to be taken for granted; theſe things having never been found aſunder; becauſe, for many centuries, as I have ſhewn, all the particulars mentioned above were unknown in the chriſtian world, and ſome of them are comparatively of very late date. Let us then examine their real origin, and conſider the circumſtances in which they aroſe; and let us ſee whether our preſent circumſtances really *require* any ſuch inſtitutions.

It is time, however, to draw the attention of politicians to the ſubject, and to compare all the conſequences which either actually have attended, or which may probably attend, each of the two ſchemes.

Infinite, as every perſon acquainted with hiſtory muſt acknowledge, have been the evils that have reſulted to mankind, and eſpecially the chriſtian world, from the interference of civil power in matters of religion. Hence all perſecution in every age, and almoſt all the hatred and animoſity that has ariſen among the different ſects and parties of

chriſt

Chriftians, for which there would have been very little food, or exercife, if civil magiftrates had not interfered in the difputes of theologians. Hence a great additional caufe of taxation, and generally in the moft inconvenient form; and hence the introduction of a totally *new power*, which it has been thought neceffary to combine with the old ones in the fyftem of government, and which has generally been placed on a par with all the reft; the *church* and the *ftate* having become correlative terms. And as nothing is found more difficult to balance than *two powers*, the one neceffarily gaining what the other lofes, the ftruggle between thefe two was inceffant, and productive of the worft effects, for many centuries, in all parts of chriftendom. At the reformation the power of the church was very much broken, but ftill too much of it remains in all countries, and more of it in this, than in any Proteftant ftate whatever. For in no other of them have ecclefiaftics a feat in the fupreme legiflature of the nation.

But though the power of the church was derived from the feudal fyftem, this moft abfurd of all its parts ftill remains, when many other parts of it, far lefs exceptionable and inconvenient, have been abolifhed. But as the church cannot now fubfift of itfelf, as it did formerly, when it overawed the whole of the ftate; it gives a vaft additional power

to

to the crown, on which it is now wholly dependent; our princes having affumed that *fupremacy over the church*, which had been ufurped by the popes.

Here, then, is an ample field of argument; and why may not the difcuffion be as cool and amicable as any other? You, Sir, have made it a fubject of popular declamation, rather than of difpaffionate reafoning; but that need not hinder others from taking it up in a different and better manner: and if you will pleafe to change your ftyle, and affume the character of a *philofopher*, and not that of a mere *rhetorician*, it will be very agreeable to us to have you of the party. You are now of an age in which I fhould have imagined, that the powers of the *imagination* would have been more checked by thofe of *reafon*. On this fubject, the *paffions*, as well as the *imagination*, fhould be abfolutely filent, and the friends and enemies of church eftablifhments fhould fimply *reafon together*.

It is time that we no longer *halt between two opinions*, fo very important and oppofite to each other, as, whether religion fhould be left to every man's free choice, like philofophy, or medicine, or it fhould be impofed upon men, whether they chufe it or not; whether any man, or body of men, have a right to prefcribe articles of faith to others, or whether every man fhould be left to think and act for himfelf in this refpect, accountable only

only to God, and his own confcience. Let us come to a ferious *iffue* in this bufinefs, and if chriftian ftates have gone upon wrong and erroneous principles, neither agreeable to truth, nor favourable to the interefts of fociety, let them by all means be reformed, and as fpeedily, and with as little inconvenience, as poffible. Or, if the conftitution we complain of be a good one, or *the beft all things confidered,* let it appear to be fo, in fair and open difcuffion, and we fhall acquiefce in it.

In thefe *Letters,* I have by no means exhaufted this fubject. Much more remains to be faid, and much more I have myfelf advanced in other publications, efpecially in my *Effay on the principles of civil government,* the fecond edition, which includes what I have advanced on *church authority,* in reply to Dr. Balguy; and in my *Familiar letters addreffed to the inhabitants of Birmingham.*

To fhew that I am not fingular in my opinion of the impropriety of civil eftablifhments of religion, I would more particularly recommend to your notice, and that of my readers, an excellent tract of Mr. Berrington's, intitled, *The Rights of Diffenters;* nor is he the only Catholic who fees this bufinefs of the *alliance of church and ftate* in the fame light that I do. Different as are our fyftems of religion, in a variety of important refpects, we are equally willing that they fhould ftand or fall

by

by their proper evidence, and we aſk no aid of the civil power to ſupport them.

I ſhall cloſe this article with an extract from *Dr. Ramſay's Hiſtory of the American Revolution.* Speaking of the new forms of government which were framed after the emancipation of the Americans from their ſubjection of this country, he ſays, Vol. I. p. 355, "It was one of the peculiarities of theſe forms of "government, that all religious eſtabliſhments were "aboliſhed. Some retained a conſtitutional dif- "tinction between chriſtians and others, with reſpect "to eligibility to office; but the idea of ſupport- "ing one denomination at the expence of others, "or of raiſing any one ſect of proteſtants to a legal "pre-eminence, was univerſally reprobated. The "*alliance between church and ſtate* was compleatly "broken, and each was left to ſupport itſelf inde- "pendent of the other. The world," he ſays, Vol. II. p. 317, "will ſoon ſee the reſult of an "experiment in politics, and be able to determine "whether the happineſs of ſociety is encreaſed by "religious eſtabliſhments, or diminiſhed by the "want of them." It is an experiment, I will add, on a ſufficiently large ſcale, and in a very reaſon- able time, we may expect to ſee the reſult of the proceſs.

I am, DEAR SIR,

Yours, &c.

LETTER XIII.

Of the Prospect of the general Enlargement of Liberty, civil and religious, opened by the Revolution in France.

DEAR SIR,

I CANNOT conclude these *Letters*, without congratulating, not *you*, Sir, or the many admirers of your performance, who have no feeling of *joy* on the occasion, but the French nation, and the world; I mean the liberal, the rational, and the virtuous part of the world, on the great revolution that has taken place in France, as well as on that which some time ago took place in America. Such events as these teach the doctrine of *liberty*, *civil* and *religious*, with infinitely greater clearness and force, than a thousand treatises on the subject. They speak a language intelligible to all the world, and preach a doctrine congenial to every human heart.

These great events, in many respects unparalleled in all history, make a totally new, a most wonderful, and important, æra in the history of mankind. It is, to adopt your own rhetorical style, a

change

change from darkneſs to light, from ſuperſtition to
found knowledge, and from a moſt debaſing ſervi-
tude to a ſtate of the moſt exalted freedom. It is
a liberating of all the powers of man from that
variety of fetters, by which they have hitherto been
held. So that, in compariſon with what has been,
now only can we expect to ſee what men really
are, and what they can do.

The generality of governments have hitherto
been little more than a combination of *the few*
againſt *the many*; and to the mean paſſions and low
cunning of theſe few, have the great intereſts of
mankind been too long ſacrificed. Whole nations
have been deluged with blood, and every ſource
of future proſperity has been drained, to gratify the
caprices of ſome of the moſt deſpicable, or the
moſt execrable, of the human ſpecies. For what
elſe have been the generality of kings, their miniſters of ſtate, or their miſtreſſes, to whoſe wills
whole kingdoms have been ſubject? What can we
ſay of thoſe who have hitherto taken the lead in
conducting the affairs of nations, but that they
have commonly been either *weak* or *wicked*, and
ſometimes both? Hence the common reproach
of all hiſtories, that they exhibit little more than a
view of the vices and miſeries of mankind.

Hitherto, alſo, infinite have been the miſchiefs
in which all nations have been involved, on account
of

of *religion*, with which, as it concerns only God and men's own consciences, civil government, as such, has nothing to do. Statesmen, misled by ignorant or interested priests, have taken upon them to prescribe what men should believe and practice, in order to get to heaven, when they themselves have often neither believed, nor practised, any thing under that description. They have set up idols, to which all men, under the severest penalties, have been compelled to bow; and the wealth and power of populous nations, which might have been employed in great and useful undertakings, have been diverted from their proper channels, to enforce their unrighteous decrees. By this means have mankind been kept for ages in a state of bondage worse than Egyptian, the bondage of the mind.

How glorious, then, is the prospect, the reverse of all the past, which is now opening upon us, and upon the world. Government, we may now expect to see, not only in theory, and in books, but in actual practice, calculated for the general good, and taking no more upon it than the general good requires; leaving all men the enjoyment of as many of their *natural rights* as possible, and no more interfering with matters of religion, with men's notions concerning God, and a future state, than with philosophy or medicine.

After

After the noble example of America, we may expect, in due time, to see the governing powers of all nations confining their attention to the *civil* concerns of them, and consulting their welfare in the present state only; in consequence of which they may all be flourishing and happy. *Truth* of all kinds, and especially *religious truth*, meeting with no obstruction, and standing in no need of heterogeneous supports, will then establish itself by its own evidence ; and whatever is *false* and delusive, all the forms of superstition, every corruption of true religion, and all usurpation over the rights of conscience, which have been supported by power or prejudice, will be universally exploded, as they ought to be.

Together with the general prevalence of the true principles of civil government, we may expect to see the extinction of all *national prejudice*, and enmity, and the establishment of *universal peace* and good will among all nations. When the affairs of the various societies of mankind shall be conducted by those who shall truly represent them, who shall feel as they feel, and think as they think; who shall really understand, and consult their interests, they will no more engage in those mutually offensive *wars*, which the experience of many centuries has shown to be constantly expensive and ruinous. They will no longer covet what belongs to others,

which

which they have found to be of no real service to them, but will content themselves with making the most of their own.

The very idea of *distant possessions* will be even ridiculed. The East and the West Indies, and every thing *without ourselves* will be disregarded, and wholly excluded from all European systems; and only those divisions of men, and of territory, will take place, which the common convenience requires, and not such as the mad and insatiable ambition of princes demands. No part of America, Africa, or Asia, will be held in subjection to any part of Europe, and all the intercourse that will be kept up among them, will be for their mutual advantage.

The causes of *civil wars*, the most distressing of all others, will likewise cease, as well as those of foreign ones. They are chiefly contentions for *offices*, on account of the power and emoluments annexed to them. But when the *nature* and *uses* of all civil offices shall be well understood, the power and emoluments annexed to them, will not be an object sufficient to produce a war. Is it at all probable, that there will ever be a civil war in America, about the presidentship of the *United States?* And when the chief magistracies in other countries shall be reduced to their proper standard, they will be no more worth contending for, than they are in America.

America. If the actual bufinefs of a nation be done as well for the fmall emolument of that prefident-fhip, as the fimilar bufinefs of other nations, there will be no apparent reafon why more fhould be given for doing it.

If there be a fuperfluity of public money, it will not be employed to augment the profufion, and increafe the undue influence, of individuals, but in works of great public utility, which are always wanted, and which nothing but the enormous expences of government, and of wars, chiefly occafioned by the ambition of kings and courts, have prevented from being carried into execution. The expence of the late American war only would have converted all the wafte grounds of this country into gardens. What canals, bridges, and noble roads, &c. &c. would it not have made for us? If the *pride of nations* muft be gratified, let it be in fuch things as thefe, and not in the idle pageantry of a court, calculated only to corrupt and enflave a nation.

Another caufe of civil wars has been an attachment to certain perfons and families, as poffeffed of fome *inherent right* to kingly power. Such were the bloody wars between the houfes of York and Lancafter, in this country. But when, befides the reduction of the power of crowns within their proper bounds (when it will be no greater than the public good requires) that kind of refpect for princes

L.

which

which is founded on mere fuperftition (exactly fimi-lar to that which has been attached to priefts in all countries) fhall vanifh, as all fuperftition certainly will before real knowledge, wife nations will not involve themfelves in war for the fake of any par-ticular perfons, or families, who have never fhewn an equal regard for them. They will confider their own intereft more, and that of their magiftrates lefs.

Other remaining caufes of civil war are different opinions about modes of government, and differ-ences of interefts between provinces. But when mankind fhall be a little more accuftomed to re-flection, and confider the miferies of civil war, they will have recourfe to any other method of deciding their differences, in preference to that of the fword. It was taken for granted, that the moment America had thrown off the yoke of Great Britain, the different ftates would go to war among themfelves, on fome of thefe accounts. But the event has not verified the prediction, nor is it at all probable that it ever will. The people of that country are wifer than fuch prophets in this.

If *time* be allowed for the difcuffion of differences, fo great a majority will form one opinion, that the minority will fee the neceffity of giving way. Thus will *reafon* be the umpire in all difputes, and ex-tinguifh tinguiſh civil wars as well as foreign ones. The empire of reaſon will ever be the reign of peace.

This, Sir, will be the happy ſtate of things, diſtinctly and repeatedly foretold in many prophecies, delivered more than two thouſand years ago; when the common parent of mankind will *cauſe wars to ceaſe to the ends of the earth*, when *men ſhall beat their ſwords into plough-ſhares, and their ſpears into pruning hooks; when nation ſhall no more riſe up againſt nation, and when they ſhall learn war no more.* Iſ. ii. 4. Micah iv. 3. This is a ſtate of things which good ſenſe, and the prevailing ſpirit of commerce, aided by chriſtianity, and true philoſophy, cannot fail to effect in time. But it can never take place while mankind are governed in the wretched manner in which they now are. For peace can never be eſtabliſhed, but upon the extinction of the *cauſes of war*, which exiſt in all the preſent forms of government, and in the political maxims which will always be encouraged by them. I mention this topic in a letter to you, on the idea that you are a real believer in revelation, though your defence of all church eſtabliſhments, as ſuch, is no argument in favour of this opinion; the moſt zealous abettors of *them*, and the moſt determined enemies of all reformation, having been unbelievers in all religion, which they have made uſe of merely as an engine of ſtate.

In this new condition of the world, there may ftill be *kings*, but they will be no longer *fovereigns*, or *fupreme lords*, no human beings to whom will be afcribed fuch titles as thofe of *moft facred*, or *moft excellent majefty*. There will be no more fuch a profanation of epithets, belonging to God only, by the application of them to mortals like ourfelves. There will be *magiftrates*, appointed and paid for the confervation of order, but they will only be confidered as the firft *fervants of the people*, and accountable to them. Standing armies, thofe inftruments of tyranny, will be unknown, though the people may be trained to the ufe of arms, for the purpofe of repelling the invafion of *Barbarians*. For no other defcription of men will have recourfe to war, or think of difturbing the repofe of others; and till they become civilized, as in the natural progrefs of things they neceffarily muft, they will be fufficiently overawed by the fuperior power of nations that are fo.

There will ftill be *religion*, and of courfe *minifters* of it; as there will be teachers of philofophy, and practitioners in medicine; but it will no longer be the concern of the ftate. There will be no more *Lord Bifhops*, or *Archbifhops*, with the titles, and powers, of temporal princes. Every man will provide religion for himfelf; and therefore it will be fuch as, after due enquiry, and examination, he

shall

ſhall think to be founded on truth, and beſt calculated to make men good citizens, good friends,
and good neighbours in this world, as well as to fit
them for another.

Government, being thus ſimple in its objeċts,
will be unſpeakably leſs *expenſive* than it is at preſent, as well as far more *effeċtual* in anſwering its
proper purpoſe. There will then be little to provide
for beſides the adminiſtration of juſtice, or the preſervation of the peace, which it will be the intereſt
of every man to attend to, in aid of government.

They are chiefly our vices and follies that lay us
under contribution, in the form of the *taxes* we now
pay; and they will, of courſe, become ſuperfluous,
as the world grows wiſer and better. It is a moſt
unreaſonable ſum that we now pay for the ſingle article of *government*. We give, perhaps, the amount
of one half our property, for the ſecure enjoyment
of the reſt, which, after all, for want of a good po-
lice, is very inſecure.

However, the enormous debts which our preſent ſyſtems of government, and the follies of our
governors, have intailed upon us, like all other
evils in the plan of providence, promiſe to be eventually the cauſe of the greateſt *good*, as neceſſary
means of bringing about the happy ſtate of things
above deſcribed. And the improvement of Europe
may ſerve as an example to the reſt of the world,

and

and be the inftrument of other important changes, which I fhall not dwell upon in this place.

By means of *national debts*, the wheels of feveral European governments are already fo much clogged, that it is impoffible they fhould go on much longer. We fee our taxes, even without war, continually increafing. The very peace eftablifhment of France could not be kept up any longer, and the fame muft foon be the fituation of other nations. All the caufes which have operated to the increafe of thefe debts, continue to operate, and with increafed force; fo that our approach to this *great crifis* of our affairs, is not equable, but accelerated. The prefent generation has feen the debt of this nation rife from a mere trifle to an amount that already threatens ruin. And will not the next generation, if not the prefent, fee this ruin?

If the prefent change of the French government, brought on, to ufe a phrafe of yours, by *fifcal difficulties*, has been attended with fuch an interruption of their manufactures, fuch a ftagnation of their commerce, and fuch a diminution of their current fpecie, as has greatly added to the difficulties of that country; what are we to expect, in a fimilar crifis, in *this* country, which depends fo much more upon manufactures and commerce than France ever did, and which has far lefs refource within itfelf?

If you, Sir, together with your old or your new friends, can steer the ship of the state through the storm, which we all see to be approaching, you will have more wisdom and steadiness than has yet been found in any who have hitherto been at the head of our affairs. And if, in these circumstances, you can save the *church*, as well as the *state*, you will deserve no less than *canonization*, and St. Edmund will be the greatest name in the calendar. But great occasions call forth, and in a manner create, great and unknown ability, as we have lately seen in the history of the American revolution. A good providence also governs the world, and therefore we need not despair.

If the condition of other nations be as much bettered as that of France will probably be, by her improved system of government, this great crisis, dreadful as it appears in prospect, will be *a consummation devoutly to be wished for*, and though calamitous to many, perhaps to many innocent persons, will be eventually most glorious and happy.

To you, Sir, all this may appear such wild declamation, as your treatise appears to me. But speculations of this kind contribute to exhilerate my mind, as the consideration of the French revolution has contributed to disturb and distress yours; and thus is verified the common proverb, which says, *One man's meat is another man's poison.* If this be a dream, a dream, it is, however, a pleafing one, and has nothing in it malignant, or unfriendly to any. All that I look to promifes no exclufive advantage to myfelf, or my friends ; but an equal field for every generous exertion to *all*, and it makes the great object of all our exertions to be the public good.

I am, DEAR SIR,

Your very humble fervant,

J. PRIESTLEY.

Birmingham, Jan. 1, 1791.